Dear reader,

At a Buddhist temple in San Diego, there is a memorial room filled with tiny photographs of those who have passed. Mostly, the portraits show people with gray hair who I hope lived full lives. One section of the wall, however, is reserved for black-and-white images. All are in their teens, twenties, thirties, forties. Young. The hairstyles date back to the late seventies, early eighties. It is not explained, but visitors know they are looking at those who lost their lives at sea in hopeful attempts to become refugees. Every Vietnamese knows of at least one such person.

On one visit, I kept staring at a particular girl. Her hair was short and jagged, her eyes intense, her lips tight. I researched what might have caused her to join the thousands of Vietnamese who escaped post-war Việt Nam. Then I imagined the details of what she witnessed at sea.

Years later, her face continued to visit me. By now I wanted to focus on what happened to her upon landing in a safe place. How does she return to herself?

I put a name to a face and she became Hằng. I placed her in a land she could not have imagined, the opposite of the lush green she loved yet needed to flee. Enter the Panhandle in Texas. I spent my adolescence in Texas, so I know of its dry flat landscape to the west.

Then I needed a buddy for Hằng. Enter LeeRoy. He was a boy I might have gone to high school with in Fort Worth. A cowboy wannabe, dreaming of rodeo glory while trudging through the halls with horse dung on his boots. His innate kindness would soothe Hằng's fiery vulnerabilities. Together, in spite of themselves, they would trade humor and solace.

Sometimes true connection sprouts between two most unlikely people. And sometimes healing is spurred in a place that reminds you of nothing you have known. Hằng begins to thaw as she gets to know LeeRoy and West Texas. I hope you enjoy getting to know all three.

To life's lovely surprises,

Thanhhà Lai

ALSO BY THANHHÀ LẠI

Inside Out & Back Again

Listen, Slowly

butterfly
yellow

THANHHÀ LẠI

HARPER

An Imprint of HarperCollins*Publishers*

First Edition

In memory of
the thousands of refugees
at the bottom of the sea

butterfly yellow

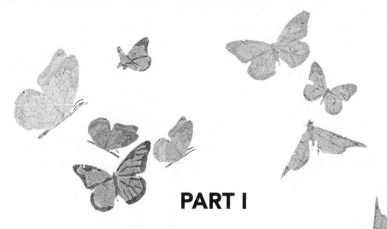

PART I

the road

Brittle Brown Ocean

On the bus, Hằng stares into the endless expanse. She concentrates on even inhales, then slow exhales. Nibbling on ginger, she's determined to soothe the relentless stirrings of nausea as her intestines coil into eels.

Fiery ginger flashes down and quiets the eels. She sharpens her stare. Having flown in from a refugee camp yesterday, she's already on her way to A-ma-ri-lo. Never mind that her inner clock still clicks thirteen hours ahead. Never mind that her uncle will be chasing her. Never mind that she can barely speak English and can understand only half of a sentence.

The other passengers spit out words in a hissy, snaky language. How they talk, and sing and hum, and eat, how they eat. An explosion of cheer and chemicals: sweet, tangy, salty, bubbly, crispy, oniony. None of it helps her nausea.

They must see her as strange. A jagged-hair girl cocooned in long sleeves, heavy pants. Meanwhile they dress for the beach. This, despite vents blowing such frigid air Hằng senses fog in her breaths.

She sits by herself and marvels at a land so flat it erases the horizon, presenting a brittle brown ocean instead of glassy blue green. Still, the same vastness, the same unknown.

Each bounce on the bus recalls bobbing on a boat. Hằng bites off a chunk of ginger. Chomps into searing bitterness. Anything to stop memories of her escape by sea.

Summer 1981

A boy of eighteen, self-renamed LeeRoy that very morning, is driving past the same dry expanse. Here and there, scraggly mesquites break up the blanket of brown. Enough heat out there to scorch every tree into kindling. Sitting in air-conditioning, he whistles, having waited all his life to reach this open plain where a man can get at his true self.

LeeRoy has driven up from Austin, from his home in the Hill Country where rolling green slopes don't stand a chance against the allure of dusty cowboy country. His confused parents, UT professors, have been told not to expect him back for a good long while. It took more than a month after graduation to skedaddle, his folks inventing one reason or another to hold on to him. A party, a family trip to Big Ben, opening weekend for *Indiana Jones*, then an all-out Fourth of July barbecue last night.

This morning LeeRoy finally headed out for the Lone Star, a honky-tonk in Amarillo where his idol, Bruce Ford, will be making a splash.

Summer 1981, Bruce Ford has been the NFR bareback champion two years running. In his prime at twenty-nine, he sits on an incensed bronco like he's on a swing. True, LeeRoy has never met Ford, but he's absorbed everything about this man, beginning three years ago when Ford won the PRCA season championship.

It's understood that cowboys don't take kindly to hangers-on. At a party though, where Ford will likely have a few beers and loosen up, LeeRoy is betting the champ will spare his number-one fan a portion of his time. LeeRoy plans on approaching Mr. Ford and offering up free labor. Mucking, grooming, cooldowns. Hell, LeeRoy might as well dream big and imagine his tag-a-long turning into a real job, putting him front and center in Oklahoma City when the man himself will defend his title come December.

Hằng

That same morning, using halting English aided by scratchy illustrations, Hằng persuaded her cousin En-Di (illogically spelled "Angie") to risk her own father's fury and drive her to the bus station. She gestured a story that her brother is distraught and waiting for her. It's been six years, two months, and fifteen days since April 20, 1975, when the siblings got separated.

Hằng did not need to explain that retrieving her brother equated to her life's singular focus. Every twitch in her face said it for her.

"Really? Your brother knows you're coming? Dad would never let you go. But then he says no to everything. You have to do this alone? He's going to be livid, and I guess I can say you insisted and cried and were going to drive off and wreck my Mustang. And you're eighteen, you should be able to go off by yourself, I certainly will be out of here in two years. You are eighteen?"

Hằng nodded, uncertain which question she was answering. The more Hằng nodded, the more En-Di started packing shorts and tank tops and T-shirts. She was puzzled when Hằng insisted on pants and long-sleeved shirts, but sure, she had those too. Even gave away sixty dollars saved for a dance contest. As a final touch, En-Di stuffed everything into a bag with straps. An ingenious invention, as the straps clung to Hằng's shoulders and settled the weight on her back. As if she were carrying air.

As she drove, En-Di spilled forth an ever higher mountain of words.

"Be careful out there, don't make eye contact with nobody. You have to do this, right? Dad's going to be heartbroken. He gave out cupcakes at work when we got word months ago that you made it to a refugee camp. Are you sure you can't wait for my dad to take you? You haven't even gotten a haircut. Honestly, you need one, bad. You haven't even been here a whole day. I'll fib to Dad when he gets off the overnight that you're sick in your room and can't be bothered. Oh, you'll save yourself a lot of trouble if you call yourself Moon, you said that's what Hằng means anyway."

Understanding half the words is more than enough,

because when En-Di talks her voice acts, her hands dance. But no matter how well-meaning the suggestion, Hằng won't be switching to Moon as though she were a hippie with oily hair and a long skirt and a tambourine, as she's seen in *National Geographic*.

Before driving off, En-Di shouted last advice: "No offense, but you look about twelve to Texans, they're just big folks. See if you can get a child's ticket. They'll go for it. Remember, your name is Moon, and if anyone asks say your hippie parents let you travel alone. This is one big adventure."

Hằng doesn't believe in adventures. There are steps that must be done, and once done, another step awaits. The last step, after six years of minute planning by her grandmother, is a bus ride away. In A-ma-ri-lo her baby brother has to be waiting. In her imaginings, he is always waiting. She plans to lunge at him and squeeze chubby gooey flesh. His coarse hair will thrill her skin, the salty heat of him will cushion her nostrils.

Her brother is the only person left from her youth. Grandmother gone, Father gone, Mother gone. Hằng never would have crossed the sea on a rotting fishing boat if he weren't waiting for her. It has taken too many years, but finally, since landing here yesterday, the two of them are enveloped in the same landscape and the same heat. The bus continues rocking as she keeps hugging the shoulder-strap bag. The ginger is nibbled to a nub. Now acclimated, every fiery scrape releases sparkles of moss and rain. Flames that had singed her taste buds now glide down sweet and velvety, soothing the bus-sick eels.

A highway sign states *Amarillo—60 miles*, which Hằng instinctively recalculates to 96 kilometers. A tingle begins in her toes; her cheekbones lift. This, despite a distrust of hope.

Horseshoe Mustache

LeeRoy drums his right palm on the steering wheel. Something called rap, just hitting the mainstream with Blondie's "Rapture." His cousin has included "That's the Joint" by Funky 4 + 1 in a mix tape sent for graduation. Living in the Bronx, the cousin always introduces LeeRoy to the latest. This kicking new sound is between singing and talking, with bass and maybe drums, while the words rhyme to a rhythm like hyped-up disco. A girl's voice and at least three boys'. LeeRoy can't make out all the lyrics. Still, it's damn fun.

> *We're gonna* hum hum hum *that we're real,*
> *We're gonna* hum hum hum *we know the real deal.*

In between drumming LeeRoy twirls the ends of his

horseshoe mustache, grown in tribute to Bruce Ford's signature look. His is red while Ford's glows a sunny blond. But some things can't be helped.

He listens hard and gets the next two lines.

We got golden voices and hearts of steel
Cause we're five emcees that got to be real.

The lyrics make him happy, and when he's happy he likes sweets. His parents sent him off with a pint of milk and a pan of brownies, cut into nine squares. He's gotten into five.

The sixth piece calls for cold milk.

The Panhandle

Texas is shaped like a huge iron skillet. By elementary school, every child has learned that its protruding northwestern tip is called the Panhandle. Yet Hằng has never heard of the pan, much less its handle.

She does know about Texas, had long been told that her father's younger brother is a doctor in Dallas. Two S-shaped Vietnams can snuggle inside Texas's skillet, yet the small country has four times the state's population. No wonder Hằng has ridden for hours and stared into nothing but white-blue sky, a forever brown, and an assault of billboards: on one *Repent or Live Forever After in Damnation*, on another three cowboys tame a horse under the headline *ACME THE REAL WEST*, then a close-up of a sizzling steak.

Hằng wonders who would eat a bleeding slab of meat the

13

size of a thigh? And why are Clint Eastwood and his cool cold stare not on any of the billboards?

Back home she thought cowboys would roam this world, kicking up clouds of dust as they sped by on horses. When she tried to escape with her brother near the end of the war, she planned on coming here, learning to tame wild mustangs and surprising their father.

It shocks her that six years ago she was that naive and silly. For years she and her brother watched cowboy movies with their father. Those humid evenings sunken into tick-ticks from the projector, as film reels looped and looped. They were entranced to have Clint Eastwood flicker on the living room wall, his tough-man mumbles squeezing through lips opened to a sliver. From the cowboy's hisses their father taught her English while her little brother practiced hissing.

Her father never said, but Hằng knew, if Việt Nam had cowboys he would have given up his translation job and put on working boots. He could talk just like them. And manage the heat. In every scene cowboys hid from the sun in wide hats, blanket coats, tough pants, and suffocating boots, all the while tugging at sweat-stained handkerchiefs protecting their throats. The men couldn't have smelled too good. Soaked underneath, sun-cracked on the surface.

Hằng is on her way to the one address she knows in this land: 405 Mesquite Street, Amarillo, Texas.

In the final days of the war in April 1975, Hằng thought she was so clever, devising a way to flee while her family strategized and worried. Every day newspapers printed stories about Americans panicking to save hundreds of orphans. There was even an official name, Operation Babylift. She assumed she and her brother would go first, then somehow her family would join them in America. But in line at the airport she was rejected, a twelve-year-old passing as eight. Linh was five, three to foreign eyes, just young enough to be accepted as an orphan. Hằng saw little Linh thrashing as he was carried into a Pan Am.

By the time her brother was ripped from her, nobody cared to hear why she lied. With so many scrambling to flee before the victorious Communists marched in, one more screaming child was just that. An American volunteer with puffy, sweaty hands must have felt sorry for her. He pressed a card into her palm as he pushed her away from the ladder. Sun rays radiated through each strand of his mango-colored hair. She had to stop an impulse to extinguish the fiery puff of gold threads on his head. He was the last to board. Hằng screamed until the Pan Am blended into the sky and left a long loose-curl cloud. For hours, until dusk enveloped her and mosquitoes chased her home, she focused skyward and pleaded for forgiveness. When she opened her palm, the card had disintegrated except for one clue: 405 Mesquite Street, Amarillo, Texas.

Returning home that day, she faced her grandmother with

a confession sinking down her tongue. Upon hearing the first three words, *"Em mất rồi," he is gone,* Bà immediately puckered her lips as if biting a lemon and was helpless against the red rimming around her eyes. After a long lumpy exhale, she concluded her grandson had been kidnapped.

Only Hằng, her mother, and Bà remained in the house after the war. They were told her father had been killed shortly before the winning north rolled their tanks into the southern capital. Her mother sank into bed and stayed. But Bà, vowing they would not become a house of weeping women, wrote down the beginning of hundreds of steps needed to reclaim her grandson. First, they must save money. Next, they must write to her uncle in Dallas, telling him to go to the address.

Hằng never corrected Bà's assumption. During the day, as Bà clicked her nails and plotted, Hằng could pretend innocence. After all, Bà did not ask, how did they get to the airport? Were there other children? Who thought he was an orphan? Why didn't Hằng scratch, bite, and scream to keep her brother beside her? It was so easy to stay quiet as Bà provided herself with answers.

But while crickets sang and Bà snored beside her, the lie streaked through Hằng's blood and deposited ashy guilt inside every crevice. The gray guilt had grown heavy, refusing to pause its relentless infusion into her joints and marrow. After all, it was her fault her brother was taken.

Rhinestone Cowboy

Stopping to get milk, LeeRoy gets out and adjusts his hat in the driver's mirror. He figures he did mighty fine turning himself into a cowboy.

As part of the graduation package, where the vehicle had to be a Ford F-350 in a shout-out to Bareback Ford and the generous eight-foot truck bed converted to a covered sleeper, his parents followed exact instructions: Texas-style white felt hat, two checkered button-downs with silver buttons, Wrangler jeans starched until white lines run down the legs, bumpy ostrich-skin boots in oxblood. Best of all, dark leather chaps with fringes. He is wearing everything but the chaps. Those are sitting in their box, to be anointed when he rides his first bronc.

Add to all that something that can't be bought and would horrify his parents if they knew: his grandpop's bareback buckle, won at some down-and-out rodeo where ribs were shattered and an arm was yanked clear out of its socket. That last ride also brought on a crushed right knee that had LeeRoy's grandfather walking up and down for the rest of his days. Lee-Roy doesn't feel he deserves to hook on the bronze prize until he's held on past eight seconds and hollered out his grandfather's name, Roy.

LeeRoy's parents had branded him with a birth name no child should have to endure: Leslie Dwight Cooper. He shivers thinking of the mess boys in playgrounds had made from "Leslie," without knowledge of "Dwight." Since junior high, he's been Lee. This morning he bunched Lee to Roy and gave himself some on-the-road gumption.

In the parking lot he overhears four cowboys talking about heading to the Lone Star honky-tonk.

"Howdy, y'all aim to sneak in a handshake with Mr. Ford himself?"

They stare, looking him up and down. One of them sneers right in his face. "What are ya, some kind of rhinestone cowboy?"

LeeRoy evens up his voice before answering, "Enjoy your day." 'Course it stung, but his mother always said if it doesn't matter in five years, it doesn't matter. He's got a vision for the summer, and he'll be damned if some good ol' boys are going to best him.

There's always another place to buy milk.

Giraffe Made of Metal

A maroon car with white stripes slices in front of the bus. Hằng's gut arches, flooding her throat with a one-egg breakfast. Her uncle drives such a car. Face bloated, voice loud, he might have finished overnight work and already be in pursuit. She attacks more ginger.

Bà has trained her to believe in ginger the way others rely on pills, curing everything from nausea to anxiety, stomach cramps to head throbs. Better than pills: Bà reasoned that ginger is always within reach—in a porch pot or at the open market. Hằng realizes Bà could not imagine a world without fresh ginger. But then lately, there have been so many unknowns that even Bà, the most practical, focused, even-hearted planner she knows, could not have predicted.

Even though Bà was too sick to escape by boat with Hằng and Mother, she foresaw thirst, so she packed lemons and plastic bottles of boiled water; foresaw hunger, so she sun-dried slivers of steamed sweet potatoes; foresaw danger, so she sewed disguises.

But Bà's imagination extended only to horrors known in her lifetime.

As soon as Hằng greeted her uncle at the airport yesterday, she told him Bà had insisted they go and reclaim Linh immediately. At the mention of Bà, her uncle's eyes swelled red. So Hằng understood in the five months since she left home, her grandmother had died from the tumor in her leg that kept her from escaping too. As instructed, their neighbor must have sent word to her uncle.

Hằng wondered if she should have felt something intense; after all, Bà was truly gone. But all indulgent emotions have long remained on pause. She has yet to mourn her father or mother. Not until she finds her brother. She stared at her uncle and repeated Bà's wish.

"Listen to uncle, the child missing, you stay." Her uncle sounded awkward in a language long unused, his pronunciation clashing like spilled pots and lids.

As soon as he received Bà's letter right after the war ended, her uncle said he went to the address and found nothing but a ghost town. He waited all day, knocking on the few houses that still had doors. No one answered. He returned twice more before advertising in the local newspaper, then even hired a detective. But the boy had vanished. Now, with Hằng here, he reasoned they could approach new options, in time.

"I promise we will try new ways to find the boy," her uncle said. *"First, you come home."*

"I must see for myself," she insisted.

En-Di's father, whom Hằng addresses as Chú Quốc, grew red-faced and gushed a monsoon of reasons why Hằng could not go off on her own. Her lack of English, her inability to read the land and its people, and most importantly, her brother is not at the address. Her uncle clenched his fists. "NO, no, *Bà not want wandering on your own,"* he stated as if it were true.

Hằng did not explain that Bà had warned she might need to go around him.

Chú Quốc alternated between pleading and threatening. Hằng presented a blank expression while mental currents began zapping. It was so easy to plot against a plump, heart-exposed uncle who blinked melty eyes at Hằng and assumed she needed protecting. But he should have guessed that the girl who had been taught to maneuver past the Communists would be able to slip away from her uncle. Now that she was just a bus ride from her Linh, no one would keep her from the final step.

The car speeds on, more red than maroon. Relieved, Hằng looks to the right where a machine is dipping its long neck into the earth. It straightens as if looking for predators then bends · back down, again and again. A parched giraffe made of metal.

What the machine does she can't begin to guess, but she can watch it drink all day. Then, despite a ready mash of ginger, the pacified eels jolt awake, resurging the breakfast egg. She snaps her head back to a steady stare. Keeps still, barely breathes. Too late. Sickness grabs her.

The bus driver continues to hum and chew, vibrating the mass of fat at his nape. Crunchy something, chocolate slabs, gooey round pastries with a hole in the center. He sucks sticky fingers.

Burps. A rotten sourness invades her air. Her nostrils enlarge. Various organs realign, blood rushing and readying for a crash. Saliva triples every second. Tiny beads of sweat bubble atop her nose. Boring, familiar nausea that clung like saltwater while she was at sea.

Hằng has just enough time to reach into a side pocket for a plastic bag and position it underneath her mouth. Plenty of plastic bags, plenty of preparation. Ginger rakes with pointy nails coming back up. Her nose bridge burns. A tell-all stench floats on the icy fake wind to the back of the bus.

Groans, hisses. Hằng understands nothing when English is spoken with such speed and disgust. An entire childhood spent repeating after Clint Eastwood, shredding grammar books, translating *National Geographic*, yet not a word.

The driver yells, maybe at her, maybe at passengers in back. Startled, she misaligns the plastic bag and the next eggy gingery rush lands on her cousin's white shoes.

Now the driver shouts directly at her. The bus-boat slows and veers off the highway. Screeches to a full stop. A rough right flings her to the window frame. Left into a parking lot. Jerks to park. The eels in her gut are furious.

The door flips open and flaming air invades, contrasting with gray ice inside. Her temples begin to thump. The slimy yellow splatter bleeds into her shoes.

The Others

Tongues click, heads shake.

As passengers march out, each gets a bird's-eye view of the girl's shapeless cropped hair. Before this nuisance, while judging the back of her head, some had *tsk-tsk*ed the type of parents who would send a mere child on the bus, alone. Furthermore, they didn't even have the decency to put her in shorts or a sundress. Just looking at her, in jeans and a long-sleeved shirt buttoned to her throat, cranks up the temperature.

One woman in all red from hat to heels says to no one in particular, "These newcomers, they don't bother to learn the law."

"That's the thing, no law says who can be parents," another voice answers.

"You'd think once we let them in, they'd do their part to not drag trouble around with them," says the one in red.

A third voice, "Now, now, the poor child got carsick, that's all."

No one helps her.

They hurry inside the rest stop. They might be from here, but it doesn't mean they have taken a liking to the West Texas heat and wind. In crisp air-conditioning, greeted by ice cream, pizzas, burgers, and a multicolored row of self-served slushies, they collectively sigh.

The driver comes out of the bathroom holding two rolls of paper towels, one wet, one dry. As soon as the offending girl staggers out and squints at the sun, he waves her over and hand signals instructions before going in search of an air freshener.

When he and the others return to the bus, each clutching a heavy plastic bag, the air has regained the comfort of sugar and salt. He sprays Vanilla Cupcake to get everyone settled.

Neither the girl nor her backpack is on the bus. He honks a faint warning, waits ten beats before easing back to West 287. After all, he did announce before they exited that those who diddle-daddle will find themselves without a ride.

Kindness From the Stomach Out

Hằng has put on her aunt's hat, wide as an umbrella, yet the sun soaks past the fabric, past coarse blue-black hair to sink into her skull. Unlike gooey sticky vapors back home, the dry air here claws moisture from her skin and leaves bee stings in her throat.

She reaches where the bus should be, touches nothing but scorching waves of heat. More grains of dust land on her cracked lips, cling to watery eyes. She retreats inside.

Panic begins its slow gnaw as Bà's words unravel from Hằng's most inner coils. *Deep breath, again, now strategize your next immediate task, no matter a heart drumming thùng thùng, no matter arms and legs softening to noodles.*

Hằng hides behind a standing picture of a sugar-glazed cake the size of her torso. The image alone induces a swollen tongue and a stomachache. It's 4:27. She must get to A-ma-ri-lo before nightfall, before her brother is put to bed. In case he's not there, she needs daylight to . . . no, he will be there.

Hằng hears Bà's voice again: *When in danger look for those who can't help but be kind, kindness from the stomach out. Tốt từ trong bụng ra.*

Hằng looks: a tall cowboy stomping the floor in heeled boots (no), a wiggly woman with big hair and a tiny waist (no), a laughing couple with hands in each other's jeans pocket (no), a father scolding his boy (no), three women in doll dresses and boots (no), an older couple, plain of dress, low of voice.

She inhales and commands herself forward despite a torpedo-ing heart and wavery nerves, knowing outsiders see her as short, quail-boned, narrow-shouldered, and without any fat. But if they look into her eyes, they can't miss the determination. If a camera were to capture her face, or better yet just her eyes, she can pass for being in her twenties and beyond.

She tries a simple "Hé-lô," but lead fills her tongue. Ever prepared, she pulls out cards En-Di had been instructed to write in bold and shoves one at the woman.

"No thank you, dearie, we don't want to buy anything."

Hằng holds up the card and jabs at the words:
PLEASE GO TO 405 MESQUITE STREET IN AMARILLO.
MY BROTHER NEEDS HELP NOW.

"Is she mute?" the man asks. "I'll be, who would leave a mute child at a rest stop? She looks about ready to cry on us."

Instead of tears, Hằng wants to shout. She feels the humiliating claws of desperation, which holds hands with helplessness. How she hates being helpless. But the couple's faces are softening. A crying, soft mute she shall become.

Tears refuse to drop. So annoyed with herself she's near a growl, probably appearing feral, an expression she has tried to banish but it nonetheless paces beneath her skin.

"Is her brother in trouble?" The man has an easy, slow, understandable lilt. He looks at his wife. "We have time to give the child a lift?"

They confer. Heads shake.

Hằng thrusts a second card at them:

I COME FROM VIETNAM TO RESCUE MY BROTHER.

"Vietnam? My word!"

Hằng nods and nods.

The couple, in turn, assesses the crowd. They settle on a husband, wife, tall girls. Before they finish explaining, the family walks away. People have been watching and are rushing to emergencies in the bathroom, out in the heat.

A shiny, tall cowboy walks in. Ripened-papaya hair, speckled face, pillow middle, puffy cheeks, and those eyes, those beaming eyes belong to someone who has received a sky size of indulgence. The couple rushes toward him.

Hằng panics. She can't tell if kindness coils within his stomach. His inside is blank to her. Still, she's careful. Plenty of blank children grow up evil. She's certain of only one fact: he's the cleanest cowboy she's ever seen.

He says, "I'm not going that way." The couple keeps whispering.

He says, "But I've got somewhere I've got to be." The couple reasons with him.

He says, "Sorry." The couple tries to give him ten dollars.

He walks fast outside. They follow and drag along a confused Hằng.

They all stop at a gleaming red truck. The wife takes the cowboy's hand, smiles, and places Hằng's emergency card in his palm. "Take her to this here address. It can't be but a few minutes out of your way." She pauses until he looks at her. "It's the Christian thing to do."

She opens the passenger-side door and shoves in Hằng, who catches the woman's husband tucking ten dollars inside the cowboy's shirt pocket. "Son, show her some good ol' Texas hospitality."

Hằng could not catch the last word, sounding like "hót-sì-pi-tô." Why would they be going to a hospital? Before she could ask, the couple hurries away.

The cowboy gets in and won't look at her. Hằng presses against the closed passenger door and shields herself with her bag. She would never have climbed into this soaring truck on her own. For one, the back is encased with a red roof and black windows. Anything can be hidden inside such darkness.

The truck's leather seat lights her back and bottom on fire, but she can't indulge such a worry right now. At her ankle she unsnaps the sheath of a skinning knife borrowed from her uncle. Staring at the spotless cowboy, she calls forth her best Clint Eastwood unforgiving eyes and razor lips.

Cold Ginger Ale

Of all things, the ungrateful girl has the nerve to be throwing sideways glares.

"Hey, I'm not the bad guy here. Minding my own business, just wanting some cold milk, is that too much to ask? Then damn it all to hell, I get roped into being your taxicab. It's not every day I get a chance to eyeball Bruce Ford. I've got to get there early to scout out the best seat. They may not be letting folks in come evening."

LeeRoy sighs, and there's nothing to be done but keep driving. "This ain't nothing but bullshit," he spits out. His grammarian mother would have snapped at "ain't," but grammar be damned, she's not the one stuck with a foreign mute bird of a girl.

He does love the sensation of words buzzing inside his

throat, especially loves to wrap them around a Texas contour. He spent all last year in the library looking up cowboy slangs. The more phrases slip through his lips, the more he feels like a cowboy. Bonus that each little saying gets a rise out of his East-Coast, strict-tongue mother.

When he's cornered, he talks. When he's stumped, he talks. When he's outwitted, he talks. Right now, the conditions for running his mouth are tripping all over themselves.

"You likely don't know, but Bruce Ford on a bronc is pure magic. See, what he does is he jacks his feet way up high for greater leg extension, and his riding arm absorbs all the horse's beating, that's how he hangs on past eight seconds as easily as you and me breathing. Lots of times he rides on for ten, eleven, just for the fun of it. They say, and I don't doubt it, he'll be the first cowboy to pocket a hundred grand for one year's worth of barebacking. Man, oh man, he could take . . ."

He's so busy talking he hasn't bothered to turn on the cassette tape. It wouldn't be right listening to rap right now anyhow. Rap requires a happy mood. He should be mad, downright furious. But he's never liked how anger plugs the hole in his throat, messing with his breathing. It does help that the girl knows to hush.

"It took me eighteen long years to get some distance from my parents. Well-meaning and all, but they got ideas. Would have loved to ship my bee-hind to Yale, their pride and joy, but man, did I surprise them. This cowboy life, it's not a choice, it's a calling that . . ."

When he finally glances at his passenger, she's mighty green. Probably from bundling up neck to toes. No right-minded Texan would ever be caught with sleeves down in this heat. Her one hand squeezes her mouth, the other fumbles at the front pocket of her backpack.

"Listen up, this here is a brand-new truck."

She does not look like she cares. He eases to the shoulder, remembering his parents' warning about getting his side mirror ripped right off. But an emergency is an emergency.

The girl frees a plastic bag and places it under her mouth just in time. He stares at her, has stopped talking and driving to really look. Sees a girl in need of comfort. He rolls down the window for airing, then goes to the back of the truck.

He hands over a cold ginger ale. "It'll do you wonders."

She reads the label, stretches the cold can across her forehead.

"No, you drink it, like this." He takes the can, pops it, and pretends a tilt toward his mouth. "My mom always gave me ginger ale when I felt poorly. She's good like that."

The girl now holds it upright on her forehead, seemingly annoyed that it can no longer be sideways.

If anyone has a right to be annoyed, it's certainly not this little missy turning up her nose at a perfectly good ice-cold coke. LeeRoy has a mind to leave her right here on the side of the highway. But he would waste more time circling back.

Before driving on, he starts to roll up the window. She shakes her head like she's flinging off a spider, points to her throat. He tries to turn on the air conditioner. She nips that move too.

He has to admit hot wind is better than smelling vomit. But not much better. He grabs the can and gulps its bubbly goodness. Burps.

"Shows you."

Without so much as a glance at him, the girl snatches back the empty can and presses it sideways against her forehead.

LeeRoy looks on down the highway. It's already an awfully long day.

Red Line Across Pale Throat

The can, albeit warmer now, revives her like a gigantic piece of ginger. She's relieved to not be gnawing a nub in front of the cowboy, who would say the root looks like a deformed hand. Then he would insist on tasting it and drown her with opinions about its scorching rawness.

Hằng doesn't want to talk, even if her English were perfect. The quiet soothes her, allowing concentration on the one goal that will make worthwhile the six years of planning and the twelve days at sea. Then there were the three days on the island and the four and a half months in a refugee camp, an unusually short stay because of her Extreme Trauma status. All of it, even the worst of it, will be erased upon clutching her brother.

A year after the war, her uncle had written that Linh had vanished. Bà then swirled up plans for herself, Hằng, and

Mother to cross the world and look for him themselves. Saving money remained the priority. They needed enough gold to secure three places on an escape boat. Prices kept rising as some Saigonese began bribing their way onto flimsy fishing vessels. Their old paper money was worthless after the new regime adopted new currency; their men were imprisoned in reeducation camps; their homes were confiscated; their children would be taught Communist thinking. And mostly everyone was hungry.

The goal was to reach international waters and hope for mercy from a friendly ship. If not that, then escapees aimed for the Philippines (the most welcoming) or Indonesia or Malaysia. Everyone knew to steer clear of Thailand, whose gulf was ruled by fishermen turned pirates. But it wasn't always possible to control the direction of the wind or the strengths of currents.

The savings would take years, as her uncle could only send a few hundred dollars annually. Any more and the Communists would record them as rich. Being rich brought attention, which brought resentment, which brought trouble.

Last year they received great news. Various countries would begin accepting refugees under the Orderly Departure Program, which meant flying out instead of chancing death on rickety boats. Too many bodies were being buried at sea.

Then a somber note. Even though Chú Quốc filed to sponsor them, an authorized departure would require the correct stamps from various agencies. Hằng's family was not designated priority refugees, which were South Vietnamese soldiers with whom the Americans sided.

While the family half hoped for the magical paperwork to get approved, Bà returned to plotting an escape by sea. By then the ploy was an open secret with its own name, *vượt biên*, meaning "escape border."

Bà never relied on one option, always it was *bắt cá hai tay*, *catch fish with two hands*. One way or another, they would leave and reclaim her brother.

By early this year, however, Bà altered her plans again. She would not be able to accompany them; a tumor on her leg had enlarged to keep her bedridden. Hằng and Mother must depart on their own because approaching danger at home outweighed the uncertainties at sea.

Hằng leans out the window, real air enthralling despite being whipped and hot. The shock of dry heat relieves her from the burden of memories. It matters not how she ended up alone across the world. She's now here, within hours of her brother.

She knows she should smile and thank the cowboy for easing her toward the final step, but first she must evaluate the goodness of his stomach. For her to do so, words need to stop scattering from his mouth like drops from a waterfall. Something about milk, a horse, and so good. Do people here drink horse milk?

How the immaculate cowboy talks. She imagines his jaw muscles sore, voice box cracked. She hasn't spoken as many words since leaving home.

The stench of rotten fish on sun-tough skin. A red line across a pale thin throat.

Hằng shakes her head, forbidding the memories. Instead, she concentrates on two red caterpillars windblown around the cowboy's mouth. The creatures might be flyaway parts of a mustache, she's not certain. Light accumulates into an orange-red glow at his mouth, offering a hairy sunset as a snack. She arranges the can so it blocks his eyes but reveals the surprisingly entertaining lower half of his face.

He says "milk" again and veers off the highway. She reaffirms the existence of her knife.

He parks underneath a scraggly tree, the only shade near a store. "Be right back."

Three concise words, without any fat. English at its best. Hằng jumps out. Ah, steady earth. If she could, she would walk everywhere. Each step pressed onto solid ground. She squats to the earth, grateful for raw, warm dust against her palm. She checks to make sure the knife can be withdrawn in one motion.

At a picnic table full of splinters, she pulls out a thermos of warm water. Every cell craves it. Her insides awaken. In addition to ginger, she packed squares of salty crackers and an orange, thinking such foods would soothe her stomach. Eating, though, can't be imagined, not when more time will be spent in this lumbering truck. Not as tormenting as the boat/bus, it still bounces and swerves aplenty.

Once her brother is inside her grip, they will share the orange and stories and breaths. She does allow herself to prick the peel. Dots of zest explode in tangy citrus bursts, an orchard in bloom, elevating her mood just so.

The cowboy returns carrying a pan and a paper carton with a grinning cow. Ordinary milk after all. Yet, how strange to see a grown man drink nutrients meant for babies. He starts to eat a brown square and must have remembered his manners.

"Want some?"

Pinch of a gooey cake, so sweet it rakes her throat. She curbs the impulse to make a face, even as he devours what's left in the pan.

The cowboy spreads out a crisp map. Points here and there while releasing word after word that conjoins head to tail into a long coil of exasperation. Hằng hears enough to counter with a sympathetic smile, but it probably releases as a grimace. Best to pretend she can't understand a word.

A crunch. The unmistakable watery crispness of celery.

He's eating it raw, with nothing else, like it's a fruit or jicama. A plastic bag full of green strips cut and washed. It doesn't seem possible for anyone to eat that much celery. Bà used to sauté liver with celery sliced at an angle, but that was during the plump years before her family shredded after the war.

He offers her a stick. She blinks in confusion. What kind of a cowboy is he? The ones on screen squared their jaws on dried beef and mounds of beans. Once Clint Eastwood sliced a papaya with a rusty knife, but never was there a hint of celery.

He chomps on another stick. "Love these things. They sure keep me regular."

She knows the word "regular" but its use here puzzles her. Not much about him makes sense. Before she can censor herself, she releases an English question re-engineered within a Vietnamese pronunciation key.

"Du ri-eo cao-bồi?"

Nót Me-Sì-Quýt

LeeRoy's mouth hangs open, half-chomped celery for all the world to see.

"Good God Almighty, you can talk," he whoops. What she said came out all mangled, but one thing he's got is a good set of ears. "Why you asking if I'm a real cowboy? 'Course I am, just look at me."

She blinks at him. "Thóc sì-lâu, bờ-li-sì."

"Talk what? Slow? Did you say 'please'?" He whistles. "A sly one, huh? Never would have taken you on if I knew you could fend for yourself. This is a blessing, for sure. Soon as we get to that precious address, that'll be the last you see of me, got it?"

She taps his shirt pocket. "Gô chu pho dê-rô phai me-sì-quýt?"

He takes out the index card. The ten dollars spent. "It says here go to 405 Mesquite Street. Yeah, what I thought."

She points to a word, "Sây à-ghen."

"Say again? Mesquite."

"Nót me-sì-quýt?"

"How you get from 'mesquite' to that?"

"Sây à-ghen." She taps.

"Mesquite, mesquite, this here is it." He points to the twisty, bone-dry tree they're under, snaps off a branch while avoiding hellish thorns. Why some people think it's fun to gather and pound the seeds into flour he'll never know. When the Comanches and settlers did it, they had no grocery stores.

She holds the branch like it's a gift, massages the delicate tear-shaped leaflets between her fingers, shakes a seed pod. "Mớt-sì-kít?"

"Better, but easy on the *s*." He sighs. "Don't tell me I've got to run some kind of pronunciation lesson now."

"Sây à-ghen."

"Mesquite, mesquite, mesquite, let's move it on out before I miss my chance of kissing up to Bruce Ford."

While driving, LeeRoy keeps having to wrangle an unruly map and repeat "Mesquite," "Street," "Amarillo," and "Texas" until his tongue knots into a lariat loop. Of the many educational and cultural exposures his Yalie parents heaped upon him,

Boy Scouts and the ways of knots were at least tolerable. He pretended to be on cattle drives while enduring wilderness survivals.

As for the camps for budding mathematicians, biologists, lawyers, doctors, sociologists, tennis players, chess champs, inventors, sculptors, painters, pianists, and more he can't recall just now, let's say he got very good at counting down the days, hours, minutes, seconds until pickup time.

The more the girl talks, the more he gets used to her way of pronouncing things. If he waits, letting the context and syllables melt together, her words reveal themselves. Except he can't get her to stop hissing like a snake roasted alive every time a little *s* shows up in the middle or end of words. He never noticed English swarms with so many darn *s*'s. Starting to wonder how he sounds in Spanish to the real deals.

Finally, they turn onto her beloved Mesquite Street. Not much to look at. Grasses yellow and tall, fences rotting or toppled, broken-down houses too close together and all needing complete redos. They get to the end of the street and still can't find 405.

LeeRoy panics. More moisture gushes out his pores. And here he thought he could not flush out any more sweat, riding around with no air-conditioning like a fool. No music either. She needs so much talking to he plum forgot to crank the radio. He tells himself this torment will be over soon enough and forces an upnote: "Don't worry none, an address doesn't just up and leave."

The girl is blinking like she's about to have a panic attack. He looks away to not get any more involved.

He parks and gets out to investigate, all casual, like it's normal as sunshine to misplace an address. She comes out too.

It's getting toward late afternoon, still bright, but the air no longer bites. He's got his Texas hat. She's unfolded a contraption that might as well swallow her.

"You fit that hat in your backpack?"

"Bách-pác?"

He pats her bag. She shakes her head like she doesn't believe him.

"Cớ-sìn thúc hát phom hơ mó-đờ. Shhsss, đu nót theo."

This girl is nuts. He's not hanging around long enough to snitch to her cousin's mother about anything, much less a silly hat.

There's 401, 403. Where 405 should be stands a building partly blown away, partly devoured by termites. A crumbling sign says something and *Southern Baptist*. The most sorry church LeeRoy ever saw. Two bars of wood nailed in an X block the door.

No matter, his work is done here, having gobbled up much more than ten dollars' worth of hospitality.

LeeRoy glances at the girl, whose eyebrows are contorted and whose cheeks have drained of color. Right quick he looks away and gets ready with parting words—good luck and you'll be fine and all that.

Spiky Memories

Muscles dissolve into waves. Her body sinks onto the rotting porch, landing in dusty puffs and paint chips and spiderwebs. At least she has the wide hat for a mat. She coils into a pill bug, hears the crunch of dry crickets and brittle flies. Her eyes shut against the crackled, entangled stench of the forgotten.

This address. For six years two months fifteen days she has been imagining songbirds and cool breezes, her brother flinging onto her, cheeks bouncing, stumpy arms squeezing her neck. She would swing him by his armpits as he screamed, *"Chị tìm em, chị tìm em," you found me, you found me,* and she would slobber out apologies for taking so so long.

Granddaughter and grandmother studied the only link to him as if it were a poem. "405" rang out forcefully in Vietnamese: *bốn không năm*. When spoken in Hằng's English, "pho dê-rô phai," the digits were burdened with the same obsession. She practiced until the numbers melted on her tongue.

The word "mesquite" baffled them both. The dictionary said it was a wood, a tree, but they could not imagine its leaves, the texture of its bark, the shape of its seeds. They decided to pronounce it "me-sì-quýt," meaning "tamarind-(hiss)-tangerine." Bà especially was comforted while repeating "me-sì-quýt," remembering her grandson's love of sour fruit, wishing he was offered plenty in the foreign land.

Their best guess for "street" was "sì-tuyết." A hiss and the word for snow.

"Amarillo" confused them even more, not even appearing in the dictionary. But they were spared the ubiquitous snaky sounds of English and so loved this word most. "A-ma-ri-lo" rang out in a singsong cadence, hinting that their little boy might be finding reasons to sing.

As for "Texas," they fumbled the double sibilance and compromised with "Tê-sát." In the raw years after the war, street talk had it that thousands of Vietnamese had resettled in Tê-sát, second only to the abundance of black-hair, olive-skin refugees in Ca-li, short for Ca-li-pho-ni-à. It wasn't possible to pronounce that many syllables without getting lightheaded. Every word in Vietnamese is monosyllabic, a compact, crisp language where the drama lies not in syllables but within minute tonal shifts.

Hằng knows she should be breaking into the sawdust house, sniffing for clues of his past presence. But she is exhausted. Hungry. Mostly desperate. How she despises desperation. When she's desperate, spiky memories pound her like steel monsoon drops, shattering bones to shoot the unwanted into her marrow where guilt awaits. In this revolting state, her memories always stir up the bottom debris of what she can't and won't and hasn't said out loud.

In rebellion she erases herself from her own memories. Braces against feeling anything.

Two monks, one older, one younger, lay pressed among forty-six still-breathing bodies. Eleven non-breathing ones had been slipped into the sea.

Cold saltwater sloshed into the boat, more groans from bodies swollen with pus-clinging sores.

A scream. Another Thai fishing boat drew near.

Women and girls stirred, smeared on a fresh layer of engine oil, urine, blood. Anything to disgust this set of robbers.

Stench of rotten fish, flashes of machetes. On board, the modern-day pirates motioned for escapees to reveal all skin. The pirates searched every hem, pocket, water jug, oil container, wooden crack. Did not find nearly enough gold.

They stomped on skin-bone men and boys. They flung hollow women and girls to their boat.

The two monks, still wearing loose jade robes, held up a stone carving of the Buddha. The last set of robbers had let them be.

This time one pirate, enraged, lifted his machete high.

Tattoos

"She fainted?"

LeeRoy turns around, almost knocking over a woman with a cane who's leaning down to set a finger under the body's nose.

"Plain bullshit is what she is." He tries to sound exasperated but his words shake with worry.

The woman straightens, stamps her cane on the porch. Dust rises. "Now, now, language. When did this child last eat anything at all?"

"How would I know?" LeeRoy senses that something about his face encourages women of all ages to boss him around. He counters with narrow eyes and a firm jaw. "I got coerced into being a taxicab. The most trying ten dollars I ever did earn. Now if you'll pardon me, I've got an urgency."

"Let's start with names? I'm Mrs. Brown. A proper introduction always does good."

LeeRoy tells her his name, emphasizing the *L* and *R* in caps, but feels no better.

"Well then, LeeRoy, we can't leave her down there to catch goodness knows what. Get her to my porch, then we'll see who's venturing where."

Any argument would be shot to bits as soon as it hit the air. "I swear it doesn't pay to be a nice guy."

"Sure it does, but it might be a while before you can collect." The woman clomps off the porch and leads the way next door.

"I don't even know her name, honest. Best to leave this to the police."

The girl pops up like a jack-in-the-box. "Nô pô-lít-sì. Nô pô-lít-sì." She tries to stand, but that's pointless.

Mrs. Brown calls from the next yard. "What did the child say?"

"'No police.' Unfortunately, I've grown accustomed to her way of talking." LeeRoy sighs, getting sympathy from no one.

"She's got a story, that's for sure, and I for one aim to hear it. Come now."

LeeRoy lifts the girl, light as a doll, carries her fire-rescue style to a swing as decrepit as the porch it occupies. How the girl is not sweating while all set for winter, he'll never know.

Mrs. Brown undoes the highest button on the girl's shirt

before getting swatted away. "Easy, child, no one is prying. But honest truth, you could use some cooling."

LeeRoy swears red squiggly lines run below the girl's throat. Why would she bother with tattoos in that sensitive spot? He presses his face real close to her neck, as if that could make her fess up. "What you mess up your skin for?"

"Ai phai *bờ-ró-đờ*." She tugs on his mustache, seemingly confused that it's attached to his face.

"Hey, careful." Some people! "I never agreed to find your brother. I got you to this here address, so our deal's done for."

"She has a brother?" Mrs. Brown pipes up. "Where is he?"

"Don't suppose you know of a boy who looks like her?" LeeRoy asks, not caring.

The woman gets flustered. "Who's asking?"

"Certainly not me." LeeRoy starts to walk away but gets a *tsk-tsk*. "You wouldn't judge if you knew the half of it. First she pretended to be mute, then . . . oh never mind."

"Sit with this poor child while I fix you all a bite. Nothing this exciting has come my way in years." Mrs. Brown might as well have thrown away her cane and tapped a little.

LeeRoy senses an opportunity. "How about I leave her here for a few hours? She's plain tuckered out anyhow." He holds his hands as if in prayer. "I've got to get somewhere and then chow down some substantial grub before a fainting spell knocks me flat too. I'm a man of my word. I'll come right back."

"No siree bob." Mrs. Brown thumps her way into her house.

LeeRoy looks around, blinks. Then he hightails it to his truck, telling himself he did attempt to be civil.

Musky Wildness

When Mrs. Brown returns with four pieces of toast, foamy with butter and jam, she sees a patient blinking into nothingness. She once was a trauma nurse, in addition to many other occupations, and can't wait to be of use.

As expected, the boy is gone. "Mark my words, he'll be back."

The girl doesn't react. Mrs. Brown predicted as much, and takes her place on the swing. She picks up a piece of toast and holds it under her patient's nose, touches jam to lips. One slight lick and instinct takes over. The girl sits up and takes baby bites.

Mrs. Brown rocks the swing that has seen her through a husband and two sons. All four used to swing together on this once brand-new porch in this once shiny neighborhood built after World War II. Her husband and sons are dead now. The swing halfway remains. No bug has been able to munch through the cedar, but time has won with rot.

The girl scrapes off the jam and butter from the second piece of toast. Mrs. Brown tries not to be offended, even though it is her county-fair, first-place strawberry legend. She waits. The girl scoops all the ice cubes from the lemonade and runs them along her forehead, then her nape. She waits. The girl sips like a bird, manages to get a good third into her system before setting down the glass.

"Talk."

The girl blinks at her.

"Don't play coy with me, I know you're busting with stories. Might as well be me you tell it all to. Your brother?"

"Hi he-rè bất nô. Boi lót-sì-tờ."

"I haven't the faintest idea what you're saying but I'll be right back."

Mrs. Brown returns with a pad and a pencil, magical tools in her years as a teacher. What can't be spoken can be written or drawn or just plain doodled.

"You take your time, sweetness."

The girl feather dusts lead on paper, and shortly after a smudged portrait floats on the page: a preschool boy, cheeks chubby, eyes flashing laughter. Mrs. Brown swallows. She thought so. Only one other child has come through these parts, and he owns this face.

Young Brother Grady had returned from a volunteer trip to Vietnam with a little boy renamed David, wild-eyed and plump, thick hair so wiry it pointed to the sky. He spoke not a word for the first month, then suddenly one day, clutching a plum not ready for picking, he spoke in another language and took a bite, puckering out his lips while eyes watered. He plucked another off the backyard tree, now dead, and had to be stopped from reaching for a third. The boy ran into the house. Brother Grady was more than sorry, calling out that once the plums ripen Davey could have his fill. Mrs. Brown saw the whole thing and was consoling Brother Grady when the boy returned with a salt shaker. From the way he slurped up the sour, salty, barely juicy offering, eyes closed, each bite sloshed in saliva, you'd think he had found heaven.

Mrs. Brown keeps her expression still. "Tell me more. His name. Your name. What happened?"

The girl writes "Linh," points to the boy portrait, writes "Hằng," points to her chest. Mrs. Brown once taught phonetics and understands diacritics, how each little mark directs the tone of the attached vowel and changes the meaning of a word completely. She is careful to carry a clear echo for the crescent moon in *ă* and to direct her tone downward for the tiny slash in "Hằng."

"Excellent names."

When the girl attempts her name, Mrs. Brown hears a long hiss and something that sounds like "round." Close enough.

"Tell me more."

Mrs. Brown waits. The story will get released in its own time. She looks down the street, anticipating the return of the boy playing cowboy, who will be mad and likely embarrassed, maybe even sorry. Dusk has always been her favorite hour, when the sun has grown bored of its harshness and is melting into a soft rose to give this side of the globe a break.

Before returning to the drawing pad, Mrs. Brown sighs, knowing she'll likely see crippled soldiers, screaming mothers and babies, maybe a burnt girl running crying down a dirt path. Wars never differ all that much, no matter how many she has lived through. Too easy to guess why the girl wanted to escape with her brother.

On the paper, two mustang stallions snip and rip into each other's necks, manes flouncing as if in a shampoo commercial, muscles so detailed they pulsate heat. A musky wildness emits something rank and spicy. Hooves pound a rocky mountainside, so real that flying dust scratches the whites in Mrs. Brown's eyes.

For a second she thinks she might be seeing things, so she grazes her fingers over the drawing, checks for gray smudges on her tips. Indeed, the girl did create horses. Mrs. Brown cannot shut the O of surprise.

Hằng writes: I wanted to see mustangs live. I put brother

in danger. I alone am guilt. I was not thinking sharply. I read of horses, I watched Clint Eastwood, I wanted to please Father. I was twelve, but should have been adult. America seemed shiny and happy. I thought my brother would want to smell it and touch it with me.

Mrs. Brown's heart cracks and her mouth finally collapses. She struggles to keep pity from showing. Often, pity halts revelations.

Hằng writes:

National Geographic, January 1971

On the Track of the West's Wild Horses by Hope Ryden

Photographs by the author and Dick Durrance II

The sky was still popping with stars as I curled up by a clump of sage on an Air Force reservation in southern Nevada. A tiny spring, rimmed with hoofprints, trickled past my hiding place. No other sound marred the desert night, and the quiet sang in my ears. I settled down to wait for dawn-and wild horses.

Covering front and back of the three given pages, the article spills forth in meticulous cursive, spellings, punctuations, and indents. Before running out of room the girl writes: I told brother I would take care of him. We would see horses. I am liar. I am sorry.

If the girl starts crying, Mrs. Brown would feel no need to confess the other side of the story. Crying signals a forward momentum, a slight shift toward recovery. But the girl puts down her pencil and stares into dusk. The dimmer the evening turns, the more her face glows ashen. It was always the poised, tearless patients that worried Mrs. Brown the most.

No doubt the child has much more to write, to draw. Still, Mrs. Brown is grateful for what's been offered.

If the girl had drawn anything instead of horses, Mrs. Brown might have ignored her patient's quiet gloom. But horses, they are life at its most glorious. Mrs. Brown spent her childhood on the bareback of Feathers, a Saddlebred mare her father uncharacteristically kept well past breeding years.

Damn the girl and her drawings and the unsaid in her eyes.

"I'm going to be in a heap of trouble for this, his mama doesn't want anyone knowing his whereabouts. But you're his sister. You got a right."

Mrs. Brown offers Hằng a red envelope containing a Christmas card with a photograph of a blond woman and an olive-skinned boy on her lap, both wearing Santa hats, both laughing with Venus flytrap mouths.

Washed Bones

Hằng releases the lady and is embarrassed. She's not from a world where people hug, much less drip tears on a stranger. Pulling back, she extends shouts of gratitude, "Thanh kìu, thanh kìu," and a storm of apologies, "Só-ri, só-ri."

The hug was a gut-force response to the lady's expression, concerned and warm and sagging of protection. So like Bà's. The last time Hằng saw Bà, she was compelled to hug her too. Hugged skin draped over bones, yet with a lump in her leg that had swelled in the years after war from a mouse to a guinea pig to a kitten and finally a puppy. While they were clinging, Bà whispered last words: *"Not a tear, not a twisted face. Remember, I'm always beside you even if our eyes cannot match, our skin cannot touch. Bà luôn luôn ở bên cạnh con. I'm always beside you. Go, don't look back, go and retrieve him."*

Hằng believed Bà; after all, Bà knew how to do everything. After the war, she fed the family cheap pig fat and garden greens and the occasional luxury of sweet potatoes. Instead of rice, they and the whole country chewed through *bo bo*, an indigestible grain meant for pigs. Bà bartered for fruit in season, for fish heads to flavor soup and also to fertilize the soil.

In their last year, when a new quadrant Communist leader began a forceful courting of Mother, Bà knew to appease him with his favorite glutinous rice and fatty sausages, along with rice wine. She was the only one to sit with him, often until the rooster crowed, while Mother hid in the back of the house.

Hằng too was hiding by then. At seventeen, she had come into a dangerous age, and Bà decided a blossoming girl must be kept from the eyes of Communists looking for wives, or worse. School did not prove a worthwhile risk no matter how high her grades. According to rumors, seats in college were slotted first for children on the winning side, then for the blameless citizens. Her father worked with Americans, which placed her at the near bottom, just one rung above children of soldiers who fought against the winners.

Even before she stayed home, Hằng already busied herself memorizing English grammar from a worn book that belonged to her father. She studied in secret because everyone was supposed to be learning Russian. She would also copy and recopy the horse article in *National Geographic*, imprinting each word into her being and imagining one day reciting long sentences to her brother. She first read the article years earlier with Father, debating how they would tame a mustang without losing their cowboy hats.

Near Tết this year, word came that a boat was ready. They left during the dry season while the sea was calm. February 5, the first day of the Year of the Rooster. Bà's zodiac sign. Turning sixty, Bà assured them her year was lucky, and with the country in a frenzy celebrating Tết, their escape would go unnoticed.

Bà knew it was time for them to leave because the quadrant leader, away celebrating the new year in his village in the north, had gained approval to occupy their home. After he moved in, Bà knew she would be unable to keep him from Mother.

The family had the other option of relocating to a new economic zone in the jungle, where city dwellers planted manioc and slept in huts and died of malaria. One of their neighbors, the wife of a colonel who was sent to reeducation camp/prison, attempted the jungle with her young daughter, only to return alone to live under a bridge.

It was useless to wait for approval to depart by plane. They had applied and the papers evaporated into the air.

Bà kept talking of Linh waiting alone across the world, giving Hằng and Mother the final compulsion to sneak to a riverbed, where they hid in mud among feasting mosquitoes and waited for a whistling signal that propelled dozens of escapees to wade toward a boat stinking of fish.

Bà had arranged for a neighbor to take her in, leaving Bà's house empty for the quadrant leader. After hugging Bà the very last time, Hằng couldn't help but look back as Mother pulled her out the back door. Bà smiled while propped against pillows on the mosquito-netted divan. Sitting straight, her skeletal hands massaged the blue-purple monstrosity inside her leg. Underneath the divan, beneath loosened tiles and beyond clumsily repacked dirt, there rested a tin can containing the washed bones of Hằng's father.

Perhaps Bà and Father have been buried together.

As a consequence of war, Hằng has accepted that she is allowed only shredded knowledge of her family. The neighbor probably has told her uncle Bà's exact date of death. None of them know for certain how and when Father died, only that he had been translating for an American photographer too near a battlefield. It was customary for Father to be absent for a month at a time. His body came home right before the war ended, a week after her brother was taken. Of Mother, Hằng knows she passed February 17, yet will never know her exact resting place. Better to focus on her brother, as she's within hours of knowing him again.

Now this lady has dropped seemingly out of the sky to lead Hằng to her brother. Embarrassed to have forgotten her manners and squeezed too harshly, Hằng avoids the lady's eyes and studies the two objects.

One, a red envelope with a stamp of flying deer pulling a carriage where old man Noël sits. She knows of him, a jovial, big-belly man who shimmies down what must be gigantic chimneys to leave gifts for children. He has never visited Việt Nam, not to her knowledge. No one she knows has a chimney, and his deer wouldn't be able to fly in a thicket of humidity and heat.

The upper left corner has a return address: Los Cedros Ranch, FM 1265, Canyon, Texas. She doesn't attempt to pronounce the new location. After six years of chanting "pho dê-rô phai me-sì-quýt," it feels like a betrayal to switch dense anticipation toward another corner in Tê-sát. Still, Hằng has to put the envelope down to tame the ascent of joy.

Two, a photograph of a mango-haired woman and a boy who looks a little older than her lost brother. It's too much. She runs into the yard, into dusty swirls and crunchy grass; all the while she hums in rhythm with throaty frogs and silvery crickets and the last calls of day birds. She hums to distract hope, fearful it might turn into a frothing mouth and devour her.

Careful, she hears Bà, *hope evaporates faster than boiling water. Slow, be certain first.*

At her feet, in the first evening shadows, improbable flowers in the colors of the Vietnamese flag. A sign of luck? On each flower, a center cone springs up like a tiny thumb while red petals outlined in yellow point to the ground, as if reminding the ebullient thumb to stay centered.

She bends to pick just one, red and yellow, the colors of her youth. As she snaps the needle-thin stem, her gaze falls upon the pointy tips of the cowboy's blood-dark, bumpy-skin boots.

Nice Guy Burden

The offer of a dime-a-dozen flower nicknamed Mexican hat, which can survive on dirt and the memory of water, does nothing to lift LeeRoy's foul mood. He has no intention of accepting even though Mrs. Brown is right beside him whispering, "Come now, she's making a gesture. A polite gentleman always..."

"I didn't come back because I'm some gentleman," he about shouts. "Out with it, which one of you swiped my wallet?"

The girl remains wide-eyed, her lonely flower offered to the air. LeeRoy turns to Mrs. Brown and grinds his teeth.

She smiles. "How else to ensure you would whip on back?" From her waistband, his wallet.

"What the...how? You some kind of pickpocket?"

"I've had many lives." She keeps her irritating smile.

LeeRoy pounces on the cash in the wallet, counting to an exact $332, saved from paper routes and cutting lawns and aching-muscle bike rides to fetch Mrs. Wilson pints of rocky road. Not an easy task in the height of summer if he were to return with melty ice cream instead of soup.

To last two months on the circuit, he's on budget for $5.50 a day. Thought that was doable until he found out it costs a slanderous $19 to fill up Red, and the prices in convenience stores are daylight robbery.

His parents, always looking to teach a lesson, sent him off this morning with too many hugs and not one dollar. "We've set you up," they chimed. "If you insist on this misguided adventure, you're on your own. Remember to save quarters to call us every Sunday."

LeeRoy aims to call collect. They're betting he'll return within two weeks. They're wrong. So relieved the money is accounted for, he almost thanks Mrs. Brown then remembers he has cause to be downright ornery.

"You just about knocked my heart clean out of my mouth." It feels odd to tower over and shout at an old lady using a cane. "Without my wallet, I'd have had to go home."

Mrs. Brown sits down on the porch steps as if she's the one put out. "You could get a job."

"I've worked aplenty." More shouting, but he suspects the

effect is thinning. "This is my summer and no one is going to make it go any differently than the way I aim it to go."

Then he notices two pieces of toast on the swing and pounces on them the way he did his wallet. Cold and hard, but they might be the best thing he's ever eaten. He hasn't gotten much in his system today: biscuits and gravy and ham and eggs before he left, a pan of brownies, two pints of milk, three ginger ales, and almost a whole bag of celery sticks, which plain wore out his jaws and digestive system.

Someone was dumb enough to scrape off the butter and jam, which he devours while on the lookout for something else, anything else. But no one is offering.

"I'll be off now, been a pleasure." He finally turns to the girl, who's still holding out the flower. "Put it in water, it'll last and last."

Mrs. Brown grabs his hand. "Sit here next to me and listen to all I've got to say. Then if you still have the cold heart to leave this girl here, I'll let you be."

LeeRoy hates guilt, hates its stubborn clutch at his throat, hates how he gives in every time. "Five minutes!"

He might as well have warned the dead. How Mrs. Brown runs her mouth. Two drawings, two names, the boy being the girl's brother and was taken in by the sister of the man who ran the sorry, rotting church and who was killed in a car accident soon after bringing the boy here.

Most incredible is the fact that the girl is eighteen, his exact age. How is that possible? He towers over her by a foot and any ten-year-old can out-muscle her.

He turns to the girl. "You really eighteen like she says?"

She writes "18" in a corner of sheets of paper crammed with tiny handwriting that he can't help but read. It's an article he read years ago about Wild Horse Annie, who got a law passed to protect wild horses. Now, that's initiative. He's nowhere near Wild Horse Annie's league, but he figures he can be inspired by her grit to work up a chance with Mr. Ford.

So the hell with guilt. He stares down Mrs. Brown. "I'm outta here."

The girl steps in front of him. "Thách mi chu bờ-ró-đờ, bờ-li-sì." She hands him a red envelope, stabs at another address.

"Oh no, I ain't some errand boy you two can keep boss-ing." LeeRoy throws up his hands. "Take yourself to your brother."

The girl fumbles with her winter shirt and comes up with two twenty-dollar bills. They are crisp and new and would have taken him a whole season of sweaty ice-cream runs to make. Man oh man, the bills are a sight for sore eyes.

Mrs. Brown has to squeeze in her two cents' worth. "That there is the difference between eating what might as well be roadkill or sitting pretty in diners all summer long. It goes without saying you'd have enough to get into as many rodeos as you want."

"Hold on, we're talking forty dollars, not four hundred. No, no, no, no . . ."

Before LeeRoy can let out a fifth "no," the girl is buckled inside his truck. The absurdity doesn't end there. Mrs. Brown comes thumping over with a bucket of ice and a washcloth. He doesn't bother to ask what that's about because the girl has called up strength from God knows where to get a grip on the seat. Her talons just might puncture the leather.

"Get out of this here truck." He tries to sound stern but has to admit the girl has nerve to spare.

She stares straight ahead like the deal is done. No doubt, dragging her out will provoke blood. He can picture it already: the girl screaming, biting, kicking, scratching while Mrs. Brown swings her cane at him every which way and hollers from here to yonder about his charred heart.

He eyeballs Mrs. Brown. "This nice-guy burden had better amount to something soon."

The woman blows him a kiss. He grits his teeth and gets in his truck, ignoring the girl, focusing instead on his truck lights beaming toward the honky-tonk. It's just starting to get dark; surely he has time for a genuine man-to-man with Bruce Ford.

If all goes well, LeeRoy will take his idol out for bleeding steaks and butter-smothered baked potatoes. On the girl's dime, of course.

She can wait in the truck while they eat. Fair is fair.

Glass-Whip

Ice cubes sink like clear sunsets into the washcloth, which Hằng squeezes and glues to her nape. The crisp cold, aided by evening breeze, expands all the way to her toes. The lady is a genius. If Hằng had this personal ice machine on the bus, she never would have surrendered to nausea. Today might have closed already with her brother flattened inside a hug, his joy muffled against her heated shirt.

Hằng dream-whispers to him, *"Almost there, Linh, within the hour."*

The cowboy is so annoyed he won't glance at her. Let him be, as long as he's getting her closer to FM 1265 in Kan-dần. They must arrive by tonight, before her uncle traces her steps and drags her back to his home.

When he had picked her up at the airport yesterday, Chú

Quốc told her while they try to find her brother, she must continue her studies, perhaps in medicine, as her father would have if he hadn't met her long-lashed mother.

"Your father gave me his scholarship. I was him on his passport. You will have what your father allowed me. A good life, a secure, easy life."

His Vietnamese rang out wobbly. Yet how he talked, all the more once they were away from the airport and driving alongside clogs of cars, each vying to go fastest. *"I read about the dangers at sea. We will talk when you are ready. But surviving does not mean you can manage Texas. Stay with me. Don't I look like your father?"*

No, but Hằng kept quiet. Her father never held layers of fat on his face or in his belly from decades of eating for pleasure. The voice, too, was wrong. Her father's was clear and soothing, like coconut water, as he explained again and again the cobweb of English verbs.

Hằng wills herself to stop thinking of Father. Not now. She must focus on the new address and on swallowing spit to appease stomach growls. If only she thought to pack half of Chú Quốc's welcome-to-America offerings—more treats than she saw in a shop: patê sô, beef jerky, durian cakes, dried persimmons, shrimp chips, mung bean squares, and a rice-flour crunch round as a dinner plate.

The cowboy turns to her, not a friendly stare. "I can hear your belly, and believe you me, I'm ten times hungrier. But I ain't stopping, running way behind as is. And you sit there, little missy, and think about whose fault that is."

Hằng stays quiet and thinks of his name, which sounds exactly like Ly-Roi, or Glass-Whip, a direct translation. She hopes the meaning in English carries more vigor, the way Vietnamese boys' names translate to Bravery, Brightness, Intelligence, Prosperity, Strength. But she stops the name game, guessing that Hằng doesn't sound much better than Glass-Whip to a too-tall, plush-palm, ill-mood maybe-cowboy.

Ly-Roi turns off the highway and drives down a busy road where cars maneuver in and out of gasoline shops and parking centers. He stops in front of a bright, looming building where colorful lines of light contort into one blinking star. For a few seconds she imagines her brother living inside such brightness, then concludes no one would call this blinding corner home.

"Bờ-ró-đờ nót he-rè. Gô à-ghen."

Ly-Roi exhales long and loud, sending red hairy caterpillars fluttering. "Listen up, we are doing things on my time. This is the deal for forty bucks. If you don't like it, get out now and you can have twenty back. I ain't got a whole lot of patience left."

She opens her door, firms her voice. "Ai gô."

"No ma'am, you stay put. I ain't fooling."

He closes her door before striding off, re-tucking his shirt, smoothing the front of thick pants. As soon as he goes inside, she jumps out and runs to hide behind a gigantic wooden horse on the dark side of the building, where a window stretches to the sky.

Peering in, she sees bodies are packed together like on an escape boat.

Python arms lifted the younger monk by the throat. The older monk charged. Five bloody lines down a naked back. A volcanic howl.

In one machete slash, a red line bloomed across a pale thin throat.

Hằng pinches her thigh to stop remembering. Forces her attention on dancing couples who somehow remain attached while slithering through the density. One elbow on a cheek, the brim of a cowboy hat slicing a forehead, lion hair fluffed into eyes, shoulders clash like rams fighting for mates. Some manage to navigate bottles to mouths.

She tries to find Ly-Roi, but in the dim light every man matches another man. Hat, heavy pants, a buttoned shirt, rolled sleeves. The women wear the same uniform, except on them the tight shirts button across puffy chests. Or they have the one other option of flouncy dresses. All feet are stuffed inside toe-crushing boots.

Suddenly music blasts out the front entrance. Hằng sees a silhouette fly into gray dust. People stamp forth and encircle what's on the ground. It's Ly-Roi. When he attempts to rise and reach for his hat, he's shoved and kicked. Bloody nosed, he rebounds to swing at the one who did the kicking. That man pulls back an arm, no doubt coiling fingers into a fist.

Hằng's heart expands and contracts so fast fear races between brain and belly. Every muscle taut and jittery, her body darts forward and her head rams into the man who kicked. His ribs dent. Silver pain zigzags from her crown to her toes.

The man spits. "You got a little girl doing rescuing?"

He's wrinkly and has the stench of sun-spoiled raw beef. Hằng steps back, getting momentum to crush him again, but Ly-Roi clutches, lifts, bumps.

"Good Lord, you're gonna get us clobbered."

He drags her with one arm while the other smashes a sleeve against his bleeding nostrils. He runs. She has no choice but to bounce along. Once inside the truck, he reverses in a show of dust and screeches.

Her head throbs. Still, her pain can't possibly match his. Dynamites must have exploded inside his nose bridge, releasing a red flood that left his caterpillar mustache matted and forlorn.

"Thanh mi pho rết-sì-quều. Ai sây, 'Du eo-khầm.'"

"Rescue? I ain't thanking you for nothing, so don't go getting on your high horse and yelling 'You're welcome' in my face. No ma'am!"

He grabs her cool wet cloth and returns it soaked red.

Her throat inflames, words lining up to roar out her mouth about how they must hurry, her uncle, her life's goal. But she can talk fast and forceful only in Vietnamese. Instead, she stares into the darkening sky and wills her temper quiet. Let Ly-Roi pout. Most likely he's embarrassed. After all, everybody saw how she lent him her head.

She counts her breaths, pleading with the universe that soon the horrors of the last five months and the blood curls of this day will dissolve inside the salty summer sweat of her little brother.

Poem

His nose throbs and his entire back is put out from getting trounced at the Lone Star, but at least LeeRoy has gotten to shoot off his mouth for a good long while.

"Is there no justice in this world? I was in line, wiping my palm so I could trade a clean, strong, no-sweats handshake with the legend. But this dumbass cuts in front of everybody and ends up pushing me. Me! And somehow I'm the one who got tossed. Damn it all to hell, I was this close to Bruce Ford. I saw his blond mustache twitch, the buckle he won last year. He's leaner in person than . . ."

The girl simply stares ahead, puts a hand out the window, fingers fluttering against the hot wind. The washcloth still pressed to her neck.

LeeRoy thinks it can't be good for anyone to keep that quiet. He opens the glove compartment and reaches for his grandpop's buckle, taking time to enunciate the story of a cowboy's heartbreak. She stays still. LeeRoy can't help himself and keeps trying to reach her.

"My grandpop gave me it on my first trip to Texas, when we hadn't moved here yet, when my parents brought back my grandma's ashes to be buried in the land she despised. Don't ask. See, my grandma hightailed it back to New York City with their little boy, my dad, after my grandpop came home that last time all broken. Don't know why they got together in the first place. It was obvious in any photograph from the old days that she was never meant to be any cowboy's wife. Fancy as all get-out in her pale dresses and white gloves.

"Anyhow, my grandpop got me up early one morning and said, 'I don't know what foolishness they tell you about me, son, but I don't regret earning this buckle, not one bit. This here is yours.' I held the buckle, heavy to a boy, as he sat me on a pony and led me around and around. My mom saw and about birthed a cow."

That last bit should have gotten a giggle from her, but nothing. Tough crowd.

"Hey, you know what rap is?"

She shakes her head, so slightly he would have missed it had the cloth at her neck not wiggled a little. He does feel bad for bloodying the whole thing.

"I can't make out these lines."

He fast-forwards to find the exact song, then the truck vibrates with energy.

She sits up higher. He plays the rap again, then again.

The girl smiles. It's dark but he can make out a rise in the cheekbone facing him. He imagines her eyes twinkling.

She taps, one palm beating a rhythm against her thigh. Her voice small but sure, the beat dead on. She starts real slow and turns into a different person, the way an Australian can sound like a good ol' boy when singing. Her words stretch and regroup, bypassing her usual convoluted way of pronouncing things and sending forth clear syllables in a down-right, upbeat rap.

We're gon-na prove to the world that we're the real.

We're gon-na prove to eve-ry-bo-dy we know the real
*   deal.*

We got gol-den voices and hearts of steel.

'Cause we're five em-cees that got to be real.

LeeRoy's mouth hangs open. "How'd you get all that?"

"Pô-èm. Ai lớp pô-èm-sì." She shrugs and the cheekbone facing him lifts higher.

It does sound like a poem. And who doesn't love poems? Why didn't he think of that? He would have kept at her but by some miracle a left arrow points to FM 1265. It's a pitch-black, two-lane country road with open fields. There's fencing along both sides, so somebody must own something worth protecting. He puts on brights, opening up more darkness. He eases the gas pedal.

Up in the distance a shiny something dangles in midair. Once under it he makes out a silver horseshoe hanging from a tall gate that announces Los Cedros Ranch.

"How about that? I done got us here." He feels satisfied, as if he too stands to gain something from this address. "You know what FM stands for? Farm to market. That's what they called routes that farmers took to transport goods to town. And do you know what Los Cedros means? Cedars—"

Suddenly she's out of the truck, backpack bobbing, jogging toward a dim light. He ought to pull away, taking the only source of brightness and letting her fend for herself. But she falls.

"You hurt?"

No answer.

"This arrangement is killing me." He hurls himself out of the truck, whose beams he's forced to keep on, burning down the battery. "Speak up, help a fella out, why don't you?"

She claps. He finds her in a ditch surrounded by shadows that look to be purple thistles, which from experience he knows have thousands of prickles. It's like falling into a pile of needles. For once, it's downright smart of her to have covered up like the middle of winter. The few thorns on her face she plucks off without a flinch.

He hauls her out. She starts to march off again. He yanks her back.

"Fine, I'll drive you on up there."

The light turns out to be on the porch of an actual house, one-story, spread flat and wide like the land itself. She jumps out and bangs on the door.

"Jeez Louise, what is wrong with you?"

He drags her off the porch and pushes her back in the truck cab. "You ever heard of this thing called nighttime, when people sleep?"

"Mai bờ-ró-đờ in hao-sì!" There goes her glare.

By some miracle no one has come to the door. "You'll have to wait until daybreak to straighten out if your brother is in that there house. People have been known to shoot when they get startled in the night, and no one would fault them. Now we've got to pull back to the gate."

Once parked, he realizes he's trapped himself into hours in the dark with her. Dread and fatigue and hunger smack him hard. In all the excitement, he has clear forgotten to grab some grub. Her stomach complains louder.

"We're a mess. And it looks like we're stuck with each other for the night." He states the facts and about cries. His nose pulsates like a heart and his back feels like shattered glass.

"Come morning, I'm outta here. You hear me? First things

first though. What you got to eat?"

"Bở-ró-đở." She hugs her backpack tighter.

"What you got? Caviar and champagne? Trust me, he's got plenty to eat in there. Worry about us not lasting the night."

To demonstrate goodwill, he pulls out the bag of wilted celery, hands her a stick while chomping on one himself.

"You know we burn more calories trying to digest this thing than the thing is worth? Damn it all to hell, I've never been a good packer. I could use some jerky or Slim Jims or chips or cookies or any number of goodies free for the taking back home. What you got?"

She hesitates but he keeps staring until she fumbles through and comes up with a sleeve of saltines.

"You're kidding me," he cries out. "You go riding across the Panhandle with a stash of bland crackers?"

He rips the package and stuffs three in his mouth. "What else? Out with it, I've been a good Samaritan all day."

He holds out an empty palm. Stares. Stares until she takes out an orange.

"Nót pho du. Pho bở-ró-đở."

"Will you cut it out about your brother? Trust me, he's got a pile of fruit he's not bothering with in there." LeeRoy's mouth is watering. "Let me at this one."

He's quick with the peel and shoves half of the segments

into his mouth. Hands her the other half. "Think what you want of me, but you have to admit I play fair."

She glares at him and acts like she's not going to eat. The citrus zing gets to her though. She can't help but start nibbling.

"Ha! Good, ain't it? Got anything else?"

She shakes her head. Starved and half dying, he has to grab his knees to not snatch up her share. When the impulse passes, he chews through the last five strips of celery and goes to fetch the last can of ginger ale, making sure to leave the back of the truck open to cool down his bed. She shakes her head at the can.

"What exactly do you have against a good old ginger ale? Fine, more for me."

Next up, sleep. "I'll sleep out back and you can have this here bench seat. You probably can stretch head to toes and still have wiggle room. You can thank me now."

LeeRoy hears nothing. Figures. He gets out to brush his teeth; lightly, to not upset his pulsating nose. She's brushing too.

"Night, then."

By the time he has gotten relief from his boots, which he's reluctant to admit look good but are murder on a man's feet, he can hear her slight snore. She's curled up tight, using her backpack as a pillow. So forget rummaging through for something else, anything else. Asleep, she finally looks relaxed, like there's good to be gotten in the world.

He unfurls the mat in back and slides open panels on the hardtop. As soon as his mangled back lies flat, and with the night breeze encouraging shut-eye, he joins her snoring.

Rich Blood Beneath Glossy Skin

Upon waking, Hằng immediately pats down porcupine quills acting as her hair. Ly-Roi is sitting on the hood, loose-clothed and blood-smeared, gnawing at the white spongy side of last night's orange peels. She's impressed he knows to eat that part, which has as much vitamin C as the segments.

He scrapes front teeth against the back of the peel. "I might be liable to eat grass next."

She nods, would love to see him chew grass.

Instead he gnaws into the peels even more. "I've been through them twice. Wasn't good the first time. I swear I've never been this hungry."

She stares at his swiveling mouth, surrounded by clotted caterpillars immobile under a blue-purple nose. Without question, his mouth enters sleep talking and awakens talking.

Back home with Bà, at dawn they spent hours in the garden in silence before opening their mouths to eat *cháo*. She would love to present her brother with a warm bowl right now. She tells herself she'll have many chances.

Hằng brushes her teeth, smooths her warm clothes, then starts to march to the front door.

"You've got to ease into this. Let me drive you on up there." Ly-Roi starts the truck. "You don't want to scare him, if he's there at all. Let me have a go at it first, sweet-talk them into offering us a hot breakfast. I don't know how much longer I can stand upright. You, little miss, can use a pound of bacon all by yourself."

She wonders if someone has invented a machine that attaches to a person's throat and counts how many words are released in a day. His machine would explode.

At the house, she jumps out and knocks.

The woman who answers has a puff of golden threads glowing atop her head in the early light. The same hair Hằng has seen only one other time. At the airport in Sài Gòn, on a man who without doubt is related to this woman, on the day she lost her brother.

"May I help you?" A kind, open face.

These are now Hằng's favorite four words in the English language. She takes out the Noël card and the photograph.

"Mai bờ-ró-đờ."

The woman's eyes widen. A boy comes to the door. He's almost to the woman's ears. He looks at Hằng and she looks at him, tilting their heads in confusion. He has her brother's long lashes, full lips, and high forehead, which Bà said was proof of his intelligence. But everything else belongs to a stranger much older than her brother. For one, this boy has tight, tough arms, prominent in a no-sleeve shirt that hangs almost to his thighs. Loose black shorts drift to his knees. Can he not afford clothes that fit?

Yet it must be Linh. She has neglected to imagine him as an eleven-year-old. No trace left of a gooey, shy brother at five. Here's a rosy, compacted boy with stubbly hair and twisty brows.

"Chị Hằng đây, Linh ơi. Chị đến rồi, như chị đã hứa. Em nhận ra chị không?" Older Sister Hằng here, Linh. *I did arrive, like I promised. Recognize me?*

The boy steps forward. Hằng swallows a knot rising in her throat. She holds out her arms. He's not flinging himself into them, not yet. Still she prepares for skin-to-skin, for simultaneous sobs, for his shaved hair to tickle her chin, for his sinewy biceps to squeeze her like metal pipes.

Her brother slams the door shut.

The cowboy leans toward her. "You all right? Give him a minute. He's probably in shock."

She feels like she might throw up although her stomach is empty. "Mai bờ-ró-đờ!"

"Family! It's not like how they make it out in the movies." He pats her shoulder. "Let me try. I'm just going to ask for biscuits, no going inside, nothing to alarm anybody."

The cowboy is readying a knock when they both turn toward a loud engine. A burgundy car with white stripes screeches to a stop.

Hằng inhales, eyes wide.

Chú Quốc is yelling before he's out of the car. "Get away from my niece, you . . . you cowboy! Mrs. Brown told me all about you. I'll give you forty dollars to keep away from my niece."

"You're wrong, mister," Ly-Roi yells right back. "I'd give anything to start yesterday all over. She's a bona fide pain in the neck."

Hằng doesn't care about their tempers or her own queasiness or how her uncle was able to get Mrs. Brown to divulge this new address. She shouts above them, *"Linh ở trong nhà."* *Linh is inside the house.*

Chú Quốc's complexion turns the color of young leaves. He runs to the door.

The same woman answers, her kind face now closed like a hibiscus after sunset. "My son, needless to say, is very upset. He doesn't know who you all are and he doesn't want—"

"We're his family," Chú Quốc interrupts, breathing hard. "He was kidnapped in Vietnam. His sister has come halfway around the world to find him. It's really astonishing he's here and he's our—"

"You have some nerve!" the woman screams. "No one kidnapped anybody."

Another slam.

Chú Quốc releases strings of spit and words, too overwhelming for Hằng to decipher. The cowboy joins in. More flying sentences. Then her uncle grabs Hằng by the arm and drags her toward his car, sounding like a foreigner in his off-toned Vietnamese.

"I have lawyer. Come home. With papers we return."

"NÔ!" Hằng replies, which perks up the cowboy.

"I'd be much obliged if y'all could talk so I can understand."

Hằng hisses in Vietnamese, *"I will not part from him again. My heart. You go."*

"NO!" Chú Quốc counters. *"We guess not what people are here. Come home. Be safe. We return for him soon."*

Before she can squeak a second "NÔ," Chú Quốc has lifted and pushed her into his low-to-the-ground car. Her aunt's hat awaits in the passenger seat. So that's how he traced her. Hằng admonishes herself for such carelessness.

She screams to the cowboy, "Ai nót gô. Hép-phờ mi bờ-li-sì."

Her uncle reverses and speeds forward. To her delight and surprise, Ly-Roi answers her call for help by also reversing and speeding in his truck. They are racing side by side down the dirt path that joins the country road. Dust swarms them like a storm. Right before the intersection, Ly-Roi gains speed and brakes sideways in front of her uncle. The low car screeches but still rams the side of the truck. Hằng could not have guessed that the crunch of metal would carry the sound of crushing dry leaves. Or that Ly-Roi is capable of screaming like his raw guts are being ripped out.

From Ly-Roi: "Damn it all to hell. This here is a brand-new truck."

Hằng has heard this before.

From Chú Quốc: "You foolish, testosterone-ridden, mush-for-brains, imbecilic cowboy wanna-be! My Firebird is irreplaceable!"

Hằng has not heard that much name-calling, ever.

"You can't make her go. She's not a kid." Ly-Roi turns to Hằng. "You're eighteen. You're an adult even if you don't look it. Nobody can tell you what to do."

Hằng grabs the hat and runs from the car, into the truck. Shocking herself most of all.

Her uncle is thrashing and screaming. His words are soon smooshed beneath double sirens. They all get out.

Ly-Roi shakes his head. "This is an awful lot to take on an empty stomach."

Hằng, though, feels heaviness lift. Her brother breathes within steps from her. He's not just alive, his body pumps rich blood beneath glossy skin and is endowed with enough protein to twist sinews tight. She needs to hug him to know he's real, then she will talk until he is hers again.

Ly-Roi, looking inside the burgundy car, screams, "Is that food? Thank the Almighty, it is food!"

He crams an entire *pa-tê sô* into his mouth while trying to talk. "Best damn thing I've ever tasted." Flakes of pastry dough fly out his mouth. Half choking, he rips into a package of dried beef. He hands her a strip and offers the bag to her uncle, who shakes his head, wipes his face with his palms.

The police cars draw near, pulling along a new cloud of dust. From the east, where Bà and Father are in their final rest, the still-cool sun fakes friendliness. Hằng scans the spread-out house, the vast flat land, the few scraggly trees certain to turn more crispy this afternoon. From the trees, black birds dart and disappear and scream and return. If birds can survive here, so can she.

The glowing-hair woman approaches, plus a man from a distant neighboring house. He climbs a fence and stands with legs curved outward like crescent moons meeting tip to tip.

Nods, pulls at his belt, nods, adjusts his worn leather hat, nods. He looks exactly like a real cowboy.

Her brother appears halfway down the dirt path, stops. If she goes to him, he'll bolt like a lizard. So she forces herself to stay, to accept seeing just an outline of him.

Everyone but the real cowboy is talking at once. Her uncle the loudest. Hisses, fleeting as fireflies, dot the air. The policewoman hushes them, creating a sudden quiet for the glowing-hair woman to command: "Get off my land."

Hằng, bag on back, hat on, walks toward the distant wooden fence, sidestepping desert plants and twisty branches alive with toothpick thorns. Sweaty, she climbs the fence and sits. Sharpening her stare in the direction of her brother, she watches him get smaller as he retreats to the spread-out house.

Bà's words float within her. *"Bà luôn luôn ở bên cạnh con."* *I'm always next to you.*

One day these same words will live within her brother: *Chị luôn luôn ở bên cạnh em.* He probably has no understanding that from this moment on, she will be near wherever his heat is brewing. Always.

She stretches the brim, trying for more shade.

Shifting on the dirt-hard ground, she stays.

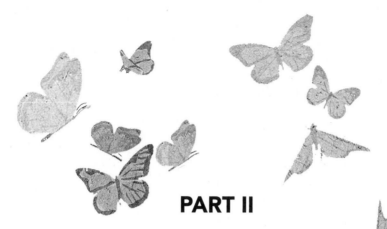

PART II

the ranch

Silhouette and Spy

Hằng has been waking at sunrise and reaching for Bà's bony hand. Before her eyes open, though, an invasion of pork fat smell and crisping dough jolts her from a mosquito-netted divan and returns her to a smelly couch, her bed since working for the real cowboy.

Outside, she scans the flat land toward the spread-out house, toward the white trim on a rectangular window that has become as familiar as her palm. Her brother's silhouette has opened the curtains and closed the curtains for nine days now. Not one word has been traded between them.

At the back of the truck, as usual Ly-Roi's bare feet are sticking out. Pink and newborn, yet enormous. She slaps their expansive bottoms.

He kicks. "Go away!"

"Hớ-ri o-rờ mis-sì him."

Ly-Roi slides out, sits on the back flap, sharpens the ends of his caterpillar mustache. "How many times do I have to tell you, say 'miss,' the softest *s* like a baby bee buzzing. No need to go on hissing like some pissed-off cobra."

"Mis-ssssssìsssssssssssssì him. Ghét ấp."

"I'm up, like I got a choice, I'm up."

Such are their exchanges since waking up sore and exhausted as laborers. Ông Mó-gần, who she addresses as a man because he's from the same generation as Bà, has hired them for the summer despite tantrum eyes from his neighbor—Co-ra to everyone, Mama to her brother. Hằng has decided "Mama" sounds nothing like Mẹ, what she and her brother called their mother, so no one has been replaced. Co-ra has warned Ông Mó-gần to keep his scalawags from her son and her ranch. Ly-Roi helped Hằng write down and pronounce "sì-ca-la-quá-sì," but she still does not understand how they are thieves. She's been studying words and phrases, adhering to a pronunciation key that needs to make sense to no one else. Her brain aches, as English has so many words. She's constantly correcting herself. A horse can walk, jog, trot, canter, gallop. Then there's the absurdity of most words sounding nothing like how they look.

While Ly-Roi swindles time struggling to wake up, Hằng

runs to get the ladder from the horse house (stable [sờ-tây-bồ]) and hoists it over the fence. She positions it to an exact spot in a grass field (pasture [pa-sờ-tu-re]) and yells towards Ly-Roi, "Hờ-ri."

"I'm hurrying as best I know how." Ly-Roi is always scrunch-faced in the morning. "It's not like holding a ladder is my ambition in life."

Standing on the highest rung with her neck and toes stretched, Hằng has been catching a shaved-head, bulky boy at his curtains. When she climbed the ladder without Ly-Roi that first morning, she ended up scraping stubby dry grass with her face.

Any other sighting of her brother has ended with her mostly observing his back as he runs away. Always she calls after him, *"Chị Hằng đây, Linh ơi,"* reiterating their names, reasoning the more he hears her voice, the gentler his memories of her.

She's vigilant for these accidental flashes, piercing into him to know him again. She has forgotten about the black birth dot to the left of his nape that the family teased was a sleeping fly. He inherited their father's exact lips, a line down the middle of the plump bottom. His adult teeth are growing out a bit forward and yellow, as she told their uncle on the phone, who can't wait to straighten them. That sounded painful but she refrained from asking.

This morning, as she wobbles on the ladder, the curtains are improbably open. She sucks in a breath as if stomach-punched.

Ly-Roi calls up, "You okay? Did he see you? What did he do?"

She scrambles down and plops on the dry, grassy dirt, holding her face.

Ly-Roi squeezes her waist and lifts her like air. "Not a good idea to sit where horses go to the bathroom."

His arms are leaner, in his face hints of angles. A warm undercurrent zigzags through her, twirling her intestines, causing a ticklish fumble she hasn't known. It's safer to concentrate on her brother.

"Hi gon."

"Naw, not gone, he got up earlier than usual, that's all."

That means she won't be seeing proof of her brother's existence for a whole day. What if he has plotted a punishment toward her? What if she's never able to tell him Bà's last words or their father's final resting place? Of their mother, it would be most kind to say nothing.

Bulged eyes, shriveled bodies sank. Formless dark, liquid salt. The younger monk reached. The older monk, motionless, floated away. A slashed robe fluttered wings.

A heaviness expands, sinks into her pores, anchors down the corners of her mouth.

"Anybody told you you're too intense?" Ly-Roi shakes her lightly. "How are you going to last to the end of the cantaloupe season if you get bent out of shape over every little thing your brother does or doesn't do?"

Most times when talk flies out of his mouth Hằng wishes his voice box would crack. Yet right now, these fleeting sentences soothe her. Even if she can't absorb the many extra words. Even if she wonders what her shape has to do with cantaloupes.

She blinks. He keeps talking. "We're right next door. No one is going anywhere, not even me. I should be at a rodeo getting my fill of Bruce Ford. Believe you me, if a grown man is stuck here, so is a boy."

Other than working and intending to give him her earnings, she doesn't know how else to repay Ly-Roi for crunching his truck. How unpredictable that the person who drank cow milk and smacked celery equals the same one who sacrificed his best possession, for her. She deliberates whether to give him her last twenty dollars, but Bà taught her to plan for emergencies, which are intertwined into life. Instead, she pats his arm then pulls back. He doesn't seem to have felt it.

Voices come from the stable, one low in tone, one young. Electricity zips down her spine. She and Ly-Roi jump a wooden fence and run inside. Ông Mó-gần has a palm up and open, the way he signals stop to his horse Thi-à.

A boy, her boy, has his back to her, exposing a slight dent at the top of the head that Vietnamese babies, including herself, get from sleeping on their backs. His scalp, neck, arms glow the same bronze from the same degree of sun exposure, proving his hair has long been buzz cut.

When she and her mother first shaved, their heads glowed like moons. Bà rubbed turmeric on their baldness and made them sit in the sun each day for fifteen minutes, as soon as the monsoon season ended. They sun-baked while the neighbors napped, then they went back to hiding in the back of the house.

On the day of the escape, Bà bound her mom's chest with layers of cloth, adding two blouses, then the robe. Hằng did not require binding. Bà clipped their eyelashes. She reminded them to always wear their knitted caps. If the caps should fall off, they would still pass as seasoned monks, having synchronized their scalps to match the coloring of their faces.

Hằng and Mother practiced shuffling with heads down, as if asking for alms. In truth, Hằng would have looked down anyway to hide mouth breathing. Already humid outside, inside the robe she was being steamed. They kept a vow of silence, thus their disguise remained intact until the machete.

Hằng shakes her head, refusing the memory. Ông Mó-gần interprets it as Hằng disagreeing with this signal to stay back from her brother.

"Young miss, go." He flicks his wrist, like ridding a fly. Ly-Roi stays. She retreats.

Ông Mó-gân calls her "young miss," having grunted through her name but surrendered. He told her it wouldn't be respectful to make do with "Hằng." He has given her and Ly-Roi rights to his shower and table, plus for her his couch. She is to come in for sleep and be out right after breakfast. Too many hours together under his roof make him twitch.

He's training both of them to care for vertical rows of cantaloupes and seven gigantic horses. His regular ranch hands have taken off for summer rodeos, much to his annoyance and Ly-Roi's envy.

Ly-Roi keeps trying to explain a rodeo [rô-đi-ô]. Yet Hằng still wonders why anyone would ride an irate horse or bull, no matter the prize. The horses are scary enough shuffling about while she plucks balls of pins and needles of thorns from their feet. Stomping and grunting, lips flapping like rubber plates, teeth the size of rice bowls. She never imagined they could release so much heat, or their shoulders would undulate like shifting boulders, yet they could be startled by a mouse.

All the years she spent copying the *National Geographic* article, starting from the first sentence and rewriting it while adding one more daily until the very last line, then restarting again and again, she never considered the smells and heat and sounds of horses. She has not yet dared what Ông Mó-gần always does—plunge his face to Thi-à's neck, sniffing long and satisfied.

She does love horses from afar. Rolling on their backs, legs batting like enormous beetles. Or bolting into the field to run (gallop [ga-lốp]) with their hair (mane [mêm]) in the wind while their feet (hooves [hu-vờ-sì]) seem never to touch the ground.

At the end of the summer, if satisfied, Ông Mó-gần will pay them three hundred dollars each. Combining both salaries with what Ly-Roi has saved, that's enough to get the truck repainted too. Her uncle, who has visited once and calls nightly, would pay for repairs only if Hằng returned with him. But that would evaporate the logic of crunching the truck. Ly-Roi grumbled and agreed.

Hằng hears laughter. Infuriated that Ly-Roi gets to laugh with her brother, she goes and retrieves the ladder so she can slam and stomp to relieve her irritation. She's the one who should get to laugh with Linh.

Finally Ly-Roi comes out, light and grinning. "New deal. We eat, then muck."

Clear, short sentences. No doubt Ông Mó-gần's influence.

"Oai láp-phờ?" She glares at him.

"People laugh, so what?" He swats at her. "Quit making

those belly-aching eyes at me, enough to give any man night-mares."

"Du si hi-sì ti-thờ? Lít-tổ dé-lồ?"

"His teeth are a little yellow? Not our business." Ly-Roi finger-brushes his own teeth. "You better back off if you want to get on that boy's good side."

Hằng notices Ly-Roi's teeth are yellow too but decides to keep her opinion inside, having been chastised.

Ông Mó-gần walks over, sees the ladder, shakes his head in confusion but says no more than needed. "New hours. Break-fast and house cleaning six to seven. Don't go near the stable then. David has rights to his horse. Been boarding here way before you two showed up. Break for supper five to six. Again, David's time in the stable. Let that boy be. He wants nothing to do with you. I mean it, you two."

By "you two," Ông Mó-gần means just Hằng. She wonders if she's supposed to be embarrassed that her brother wants no contact with her. Still, a grin enlarges. She immediately begins plotting how to spy on her brother twice a day.

Trouble

LeeRoy wastes no time mopping up his plate. Biscuits and gravy, eggs all kinds of ways, bacon and sausage, cornbread, and the best part, cinnamon buns in a skillet. He downs half the pan, not minding one bit there's no icing. Always, bunches of bananas. But he better be sure to put the peels in their own compost bin. From the way Mr. Morgan explained it, Lord help the dummy who forgets.

However many chores Mr. Morgan heaps on them, he sorta makes it up to them at breakfast. His suppers, though, need desperate fiddling. Always steaks or beef stew, both with potatoes.

"The usual today, sir?"

"Horses. Check for thorns. Infections. Water the canta-loupes. Shake leaves, fruit. Check for mildew. Rotate chickens' trailers, get eggs. Hammock baby cantaloupes. Walk pastures for holes. Damn prairie dogs. Not one horse will break a leg. Mend fences. After supper, oil more tack.'"

It still amazes LeeRoy that what can be summed up in about a minute actually torments two workers from sunup to sundown. LeeRoy has never asked so much of his feet and hands and back for so many hours in a single day. A bale of hay weighs half of him, and each time he hauls hemp straw he about quits. A wheelbarrow filled with muck, even though he's just pushing, makes him feel like he's compacted down an inch or two. Add to that the endless handling of pitchforks, buckets, pails, shovels, scoops. He'll never again look at any object that can hold any amount of anything and not instantly start to sweat. And let's not talk about the pure evil of a post hole digger. Even asleep, he can feel every one of his bones jangling against shredded muscles.

Imagine, he used to sit in air-conditioning and read about cowboy life and copy down cowboy lexicon. Back then he couldn't live his true life yet, but he did his damnedest to sound the part. Remembering to switch "can't" to "cain't." Problem was, in a university town, there weren't any real deals to practice Texas talk with. He's not one hundred percent sure he's saying everything right. But he's got to be earning points for a genuine attempt.

While reading, whenever he felt like it, he would mosey over to the refrigerator or pantry, gather up an unlimited amount and variety of snacks, then go back to the couch and chew until he was bursting. He's got a drop-on-your-knees hankering for nachos, even a worse one for brownie sundaes. But reality means making do with gobs of honey on cornbread.

LeeRoy used to be embarrassed by his parents' soft academic hands, shooing them to go gather up grit and callouses and aches. Now he's got all that in abundance and feels only exhaustion and hunger. Within an hour of eating, he needs to fill his belly again. He wraps up the table's leftovers for lunch with Hằng. That's the best thing about her—she leaves most of lunch for him.

Hằng gets up. So does Mr. Morgan, no doubt heading out to pet chores he surely likes more than people. Those would be his windmill and empty plastic trash cans he calls rain barrels.

Throughout the day Mr. Morgan will pop up all the sudden to demonstrate a chore that needs extra tending. When he's done showing them something, like the art of mucking, using not more than ten words, they are expected to separate soiled hemp from clean hemp and not waste one smashed-up straw. They work harder because they know he's hovering, from where LeeRoy cannot fathom.

In the beginning, when still trying to get Mr. Morgan talking, LeeRoy asked if hemp was legal. The answer: "Don't know, don't care."

Jack, the delivery man, was much better at spilling his guts. "Your Mr. Morgan is getting bedding for free, he could be a little more grateful. My buddy's betting on hemp straw catching on. No dust, no chemicals, and no good for chomping. And does it absorb! You can have a walk-around horse and still spread just a little more after mucking. It's probably illegal to grow, but nobody is gonna call the sheriff."

LeeRoy shook Jack's hand and patted him on the back.

He almost choked on cornbread the first time he saw Hằng changed into work clothes. The pants have to be rolled up and rope tied at the waist. The boots are probably stuffed with socks. Even though they suffer under the full sun every day, she insists on buttoning her long-sleeved shirt to the very top. And let's not forget the ridiculous hat.

"You're something to behold, that's for sure."

"Gô nao!"

She's loud for a little bird. Lately this ranch food has filled her out a little, and when the low sun hits just right, muting her usual crabby self, she's not half bad to look at. Not cute, she's never cute, but pretty in an intense way. He's never seen anyone with cheekbones sharp as flints, and those plump lips, well, he doesn't quite know how to put it. He sneaks glances her way, especially when her eyes are off somewhere he can't reach.

"Hang on, we can't be out there until seven, Hằng." Lee-Roy can't help these puns. The more he thinks about her lips, the more he feels the need to toy with her.

She glares extra hard, having told him so many times the pesky little marks above the *a* change the meaning from "cave" (Hang) to "moon" (Hằng).

"If you want people to say it right, don't be spelling it exactly the same."

Then he feels bad for the bad logic. "Fine, I'll do the damn house chores."

She leaves right quick. He swears he caught a dirty look. Whenever she manages to rile him he still can't understand what possessed him to turn Red into a punching bag. He felt every crunch as if it were his own bones.

When LeeRoy makes it to the stable, dressed in better fitting but identical dirty pants and boots, Rocket and Gracie are trying at the last bit of green grass at the far edge of their pasture. They're his favorites, easy keepers with no meds, no arthritis, no hoof fungus, and no mucking. They spend all their hours outdoors, like horses should. But the other four each get a stall at night and turnout into separate fields because their owners don't want them mingling. Then there's Thea, the bossy boss, who tops them all with requirements only Mr. Morgan can tend to. Good, one chore off LeeRoy's list.

It goes without saying all seven are American quarter horses, bred for handling cattle and general sturdiness. Mr. Morgan goes on and on about Thea's compact body with a broad chest, deep girth, short back, well-sprung ribs, and powerful loins. He races her alone over short distances to feel her ripples. For sure he won't board any other kind on his ranch, especially fancy show horses that prance around and get on his nerves.

Handing LeeRoy a pitchfork, Hằng is downright bouncy.

"What the devil's gotten into you?" He likes it better when she's brooding, when he can predict which cranky expression will hold tight on her face.

She ignores him, that's a first, and loads up the wheelbarrow. Her cheekbones have lifted to buoys. They make his insides feel funny. "Don't be courting trouble for us, whatever you're whipping up in that live-wire brain of yours, don't do it."

He might as well be warning the empty stalls.

Eyeing a Mirror

Peewee football practice let out late today. By the time David bikes to the stable, it's already 5:15. He'll only get in a half-hour ride before cooling and grooming. That's not nearly long enough. But he'll make it worse by fussing. Mr. Morgan will mumble that his stable hands have evening chores starting at six sharp. And his mom will make good on her threat to use boarding two miles away, even if they have to pay. David would waste more time biking over.

David rubs his horse's neck and sniffs long and deep. He can't ever tire of smelling salt and sweat and earth and grass. She's the first thing that truly belonged to him. And he in turn felt as if he belonged here. He had been told his dad adopted him from a country at war. But then his dad died and Aunt Cora became his mama. People were sad at the funeral, but

David didn't feel sad. The way he didn't remember feeling sad about his first family. He felt more hollow, waiting for something to fill the space in his stomach.

It was a spring morning in second grade when a foal walked up to him. David was standing at the fence like he always did before the bus came, watching Mr. Morgan's horses. A bay trotted out. A newborn exactly like her followed. David climbed the fence, which he was forbidden to do, and walked toward the foal. She put out new legs toward him. They met eye to eye. David put his arms around the foal's soft neck. That was his first smell of her. Of new skin and sunlight and home. The bus honked. But he stood there feeling like this foal was meant to make it up to him for being put here without his Bà, father, mother, sister. They had become vapors, shapes he couldn't catch. He did remember their smells. Bà was mint, father ash, mother flowers, and sister ripe fruit.

Now this crazy-hair girl wants to be his sister. She probably doesn't smell like fruit and he's not gonna get close enough to find out. Her eyes are always piercing into him, wanting something. She makes him nervous. She makes his mama furious. If she were truly his sister, wouldn't he remember her? Maybe if he keeps ignoring her, she'll leave by the end of the summer and won't threaten the way he likes things.

Mama tried to buy the foal, but Mr. Morgan wouldn't

hear of it. He said if David tended to it and stayed ahead on schoolwork and listened to his mama, then the newborn was his. David got to name her Linh and has tended to her every day since that first hug.

David wonders if he might have to drop football to get in more riding time. His mother already tried to give him money to quit, forever nagging that one hit in the head would do him in. He hasn't a clue where she gets her ideas.

But the thought of quitting makes his stomach flip so hard he can hardly cinch the saddle. He can't give up football, not if he aims to try out for JV then on to varsity one day. That means getting out there four hours a day; sprints, squats, hits, no excuses, no complaining of the heat. Half of the time, like right now, he can't get his football pants off for the sweating.

Linh licks his hands and neck and face for salt, even if a block sits out for all to use. Then she rummages his armpits and stomach and chest, looking for peppermint. David usually hides one in his clothes and makes her fish for it. Out in the field, all David has to do is crinkle the wrapping and she'll come trotting over. "Sorry girl, I didn't get to get back into barn clothes. I'll bring two in the morning." Linh nickers that she accepts the deal.

Next up, David checks for thorns and burrs wedged in her shoes. This is something the stable hands should do. But

Mama told Mr. Morgan the two scalawags were not to touch Linh. David doesn't really mind LeeRoy, who had smart things to say about White and the coming Cowboys season.

But the girl, it's weird that she looks like him. When he first saw her, it was a shock to remember that he too was born of straight black hair and a tan. No one around these parts reminds him of his coloring. It's not like he walks around eyeing a mirror all day.

As he mounts Linh, who knows to stand super still, David has a feeling someone is watching. He looks, but it's just horses doing their thing. Once he and his horse get on the trail, nothing else matters.

David tries to walk Linh, like he's supposed to, before working up to a trot. But Linh is raring to go. The sun is cooling down but it's still plenty hot as heat rises from the ground and dumps from above. Linh soon tires and walks. She has a bad habit of stepping on cacti, as if she likes getting stabbed. And those mesquite thorns get just about everybody. David tries to steer her around a prickly pear. But Linh keeps wanting to keep her nose on the ground, investigating something or other.

A rattle rings out clear as can be. Linh rears her head and squeals like she's dying. David turns her around and gallops back, screaming "rattlesnake" over and over until they see Mr.

Morgan up ahead. His stance wide, both arms up, waving and yelling, "Whoa girl, whoa." Linh stops. David can feel his and Linh's hearts, both beating like drum solos.

Mr. Morgan takes the reins while LeeRoy helps David down. They strip the saddle and blanket and grab dry cloths.

"Easy now," Mr. Morgan says. David is not sure if he means him or Linh.

"It got her good." Mr. Morgan points to two tiny holes an inch apart back from the nostrils, already red and swelled up like a cereal bowl, but not bleeding. He calls to LeeRoy, "The vet, quick. She's breathing fine, so that's good."

David rubs and rubs Linh's neck and legs. Without a cooldown, she's wet and rippling. But she's got to stay still so the venom won't spread. He shouldn't have ridden her so hard after the bite, but no one is going to yell at him about it now.

David has an idea and runs off, returning with ice cubes.

Mr. Morgan shakes his head. "She's not going to let you, son. She's in pain, not wanting ice or anything else near her nose. Go on and eat that ice and feel better."

David nods, can't speak. He crunches ice while running the cloth up and down Linh's neck. He leans into her, that smell of safety, of Mama's chicken 'n' dumpling, of pizza for breakfast. Linh's sweet sweat. He thinks about how he's gotta do some fast talking to get to stay the night beside her.

Fuzzy Mix

Standing behind the stable, spying through a spoon-carved hole, Hằng uses a fork to slash another mark on the wood. Twelve.

For twelve days now, Linh the Boy has left the stable only to get food and bathe then return with more red-and-white candies in noisy wrappers. It makes her jealous, the hide-and-seek game boy and horse play. The horse always finds the candy, even in her brother's boot. Then the gigantic animal closes its eyes as if crunching a dream, a thick-slab tongue swirling among toothy crevices to savor every last sweetness.

The longer the brown horse with black legs takes to recover, the longer Hằng can be near her brother. She has spied enough to know Linh's going to be taller than their father. When her brother smiles, Hằng's heart jumps, remembering their father's expression every time she handed him a drawing. A canary, a panda, a cluster of *trái chôm chôm*, a fruit that looks like hairy red eggs but opens to white cushiony watery sugary summer. She and Linh have their mother's eyelashes, so thick and long Bà called them feathers. Despite a trimming the day of the escape, Hằng's eyelashes are back to full length. Her hair is taking much longer, just reaching her nape and spiking up all over her head.

When her brother leaves the stable, she waits a few beats before following him into the house. Ly-Roi is there, eating. Her brother talks to Ly-Roi while packing himself breakfast. Then he's gone. Not a word between sister and brother yet. As soon as they talk, Hằng will explain and apologize, then ask why he loaned his name to a horse. Every time she calls out "Linh," the horse is the one to lift its head. Her brother answers to another name, around which her tongue has not yet contorted.

Because of Linh the Boy, she is banished from horse care, thus the stable. Co-ra agreed to let the boy interact with Ly-Roi, but not Hằng. Chú Quốc's lawyer sent Co-ra a letter that had her stomping up and down while Ông Mó-gần nodded.

Hằng takes a deep breath and smiles at Ly-Roi. She gives him her crispy fatty salty pork strips, working up to asking, again, that he please maneuver her brother near her.

Ly-Roi chews as he shakes his head. "You're spooking him, you're pushing so hard. Let him come to you like a horse. He'll train himself."

Hằng has to look away to not glare at Ly-Roi. So annoying, lecturing her as if he knows about horses. She's never seen him sniff a horse's neck or ride one or even admire them from afar like she does. What kind of a cowboy is he?

It takes control to not question his credentials out loud. Instead she tries a sly way of finding out how many more days she has left for spying.

"Hó-sì síc pho hao long mo?"

"I'd say a day or two, then that boy can sleep back at home. I've never seen anyone moon over a horse like that."

Only two days left? She shoves her share of sweet sticky bread toward Ly-Roi. A huge smile so he'll let her help with horses, let her near her brother.

"Ai hép-phờ hó-sì."

"I've got help. David mucks so clean anyone can sleep in those stalls."

She firms her voice. "*AI HÉP-PHỜ!*"

"Temper!" He shakes his head. "Have it your way, go ahead and help. See if I care when Mr. Morgan chews you out."

She must have heard wrong. Ông Mó-gần would not want to chew and spit her out. Half the phrases Ly-Roi says

119

evaporate into nothingness, even when Hằng makes him write them down. No matter, she needs to understand only a third of his words to get his meaning. Maybe his excessive talking equates to slowing down English for her.

Aside from talking, Ly-Roi does have a skill in deciphering the thoughts of others. He says Co-ra's father and Ông Mó-gần were best friends and now the older rancher watches over his neighbor like a daughter. Ông Mó-gần, whose grandfather was the first black landowner in town, keeps hoping his lawyer son will return from Chi-ca-go and take over the ranch.

If Ly-Roi really tries, Hằng knows he can get her brother to listen to her. The boys have an easy presence, often talking about nothing, but it adds up to something. Laughing, punching each other in the arm, Ly-Roi bending down so Linh can reach. It's not fair. She can punch too.

Going toward the chickens, she marvels at their easy care. They are clean, provide huge, warm eggs, and follow her like schoolchildren to a different horse-waste pile every day. Thus the chickens fertilize all the fields. Each of the twenty-eight hens has her own oddity. One struts, one flies-lands-flies-lands, one scratches Hằng's boots determined to uncover worms. Every sunset, the hens know to march up the doll-sized ladder to their house, and Hằng latches the tiny door. Ông Mó-gần has no use for a rooster.

Next she checks the cantaloupe boxes. Ông Mó-gân is growing a hundred plants in twenty-five deep rectangles. Easier to water, prune, and nurse. The vines climb on steel wire attached to steel poles. She presses an index finger into the soil and feels wetness half a knuckle down. No watering today. In fact, she rarely has to water them at all.

She also will not have to shake the leaves and fruit to prevent mildew. She tried to tell Ông Mó-gân this hotter-than-Sài-Gòn sun will burn off drops. But he stared at her, eyebrows zigzagging like lightning flashes. She looked away and hasn't spoken to him since.

Next she plucks off leaves with even the tiniest dot of white powder mildew. The leaves go into a paper bag, to be burned far from the garden. No matter her vigilance, though, Ông Mó-gân will somehow find a white-spotted leaf. She also pinches off recent baby cantaloupes. Rule is three fruit to a vine so each can thrive.

Only when she has made a hammock from stretchy cloth for each unsupported toddler melon can she tend to her own box, which she and Ly-Roi built. She added crushed eggshells and chicken waste to aged compost and dreamed of leafy greens. Never has she gone so long without eating vegetables. Even on the island she ate seaweed. Weeks of meaty, weighty food have scattered her digestion. Her uncle did bring carrots, lettuce, and unknown greens. She devoured them raw. The seeds he brought, at her asking, made her squeal. Especially celery and mustard greens. She also pressed into the soil stubs of ginger found in her bag, in hopes that the stubs will sprout long leaves and spread enough rhizomes to calm her belly for months. She waters and waits.

When Chú Quốc visited, he also brought papers needing her signature. One day soon she is to tell the story of her brother's kidnapping to a lawyer. Then she and Linh should be able to stand before a judge who will decide if they should become their uncle's children.

Maybe there will not be a need for a lawyer, or a judge. Maybe she can convince her brother to come live at their uncle's. Maybe she will not have to confess what actually happened at the airport.

Hằng calms her heart as she approaches the stable. Such an easy word to remember now, "stable," a snake inside a table reminds her of a horse inside its house. She hides by the frame of a huge wooden hanging door. Linh the Boy has his back to her, brushing Linh the Horse. How smooth need a horse be?

In mind-talks with her brother, she asks about his horse. About school. About the game he plays while wearing pants that cling to his skin. Even-hearted topics. She won't overwhelm him with raw details of the last six years, not yet. She'll tell him about Bà. He'd want to know that Bà saved a fruit in season for him each day under the altar. If nothing else, she and her brother can talk about fruit from home.

Ly-Roi sees her and pretends he's flicking a fly, signaling she should wait by the door. She's close enough to see the short spikes on Linh's head. She yearns to rub it, to feel baby needles tickle her palm.

Her brother is telling Ly-Roi, "Mama hates football but is making me start back up tomorrow. I don't mean to hurt your feelings but Mama thinks you're bad for me. Not you, really, but the girl."

Hằng's heart inflames. She's his older sister, not some girl. She steps forward, but Ly-Roi rubs his hair and shakes out a signal for "stay." Perhaps if she gently approaches, stands still until her brother is accustomed to her heat, then she can explain, she can plead.

Ly-Roi is good at keeping her brother talking. "What you got against her?"

"It's what she might do." The boy puts his cheek to the horse's warm neck. "Mama said she never got the adoption put in her name. But she's my mom. I like it here. I live here. That girl is trying to make a mess of everything."

Hằng backs away from the stable. In Ly-Roi's slight smile she spots a soft quiver, an understanding that her brother's words hurt.

She runs to the vertical rows. Hides behind her hat. No one

should see her chest heave then drop, again and again. A fuzzy mix circulates—sadness for herself that Linh doesn't want to leave, happiness for him that he wishes to stay.

But he can't stay. An angry knot inflates in her throat.

She will force her brother to understand. In saving for passage on a boat, she and Bà and their mom gave up even pork fat. Her craving for fat was so intense that when she smelled it sizzling from next door, she couldn't stop tears. When Chú Quốc sent vitamin C for family use, Bà sold one tablet at a time because that was all people could afford. Bà would not even spend for thread, instead used unraveled fiber from an old tablecloth.

In the years when Hằng went to school, she chanted the patriotic slogans of Hồ Chí Minh, *"It was patriotism, not communism, that inspired me,"* and *"Nothing is more precious than independence and liberty."* At night, though, she devoured English sentences, readying her brain for a foreign land.

Once Linh knows, he'll come away with her. Her stories will fill the rest of their days.

Immediately she corrects herself. She would never burden him with all her stories.

Midnight Rodeo

The problem with blabbers is that they blab. There's no reason why Jack the hemp man should have mouthed off about a ghost rodeo in front of David. How's a kid supposed to resist the call of riders popping up in a random field in the dead of night?

It's downright pesky to have the boy underfoot all the time. His horse is cured; even the skin sloughing around her nose has completely healed. But David keeps coming by even if he's not allowed to sleep in the stall anymore. Mr. Morgan doesn't mind, so LeeRoy has no cause to change things.

Since David heard talk of the damn rodeo, it's been nonstop nagging. He'll muck for the rest of the summer, he'll sneak sweets to LeeRoy, he'll shine up Red, he'll brush every horse, he'll pay for the gas, he's real sad he doesn't have a daddy. Geez, that kid. Cora, apparently, never romanced another after her sweetheart was killed in Vietnam.

LeeRoy tried to look mean every time he said it. "No, you cain't go, your mom would brand me right quick."

He also lied. Told the kid the rodeo has been changed to next week. That leads to the next headache, H. No more turning himself into a parrot practicing this impossible Hằng not Hằng business. She's H.

He started in on her at morning chores. "My mom and dad, they're gonna be near here after supper. I'm thinking about driving over to say hey."

H nodded. Not at all interested. She seems too quiet these days. Always scratching in that palm-sized vocabulary notebook, except she's no longer hacking English words into unrecognizable bits. He sneaked and saw a long list, written in a language that tricks him into thinking he can pronounce it, but he cain't. He has tried, given up, and made peace with it.

When they met on the porch for lunch, he added another setup. "I won't get back till real late. See you in the morning?"

He braced for questions. But she nodded again. So agreeable. What's up with her? He did ask what she was writing.

"Sì-to-ri pho mai bờ-ró-đờ."

Her list is at 136. That poor kid, he's going to get earfuls of stories.

By supper, he told Mr. Morgan about going out, and all was set. It is Saturday night, after all. LeeRoy did the evening mucking by himself, which took time, and now finally he gets to clean up for something he was born to do. He's wearing his good clothes, supposedly to please his folks, but he's not about to show up at a rodeo looking like a hired hand. He does clean up nice.

Red's smashed side doesn't seem half bad in the dark. Lee-Roy gets in, eyes his cowboy self in the rearview, then about jumps out of his boots. David is sitting in the passenger seat like nothing in the world is at odds.

"What the hell?" LeeRoy can barely contain the choice words running through his mind.

The little brat has cowboyed up in jeans and boots and hat, saying, "I figured you were lying. Don't have to worry about me. I'll be real quiet."

LeeRoy looks around for something to throw, but he doesn't want to hurt Red. "Out, OUT, I mean it."

"Please, I'm never going to get another chance."

"OUT!"

"I'll do whatever." The boy puts up prayer hands. "I'll pull every last thorn on them horses, I'll . . ."

"OUT!"

The boy slaps his thighs, determined. "Fine, I'll talk to her."

LeeRoy does a double take. "Talk how?"

"Just talk." The boy sounds testy.

"Are you agreeing to one time or every day, and for how long?"

"Lunch, I guess. It has to be while Mama is at work, and I do it until school starts."

The boy has an answer for everything. LeeRoy eyeballs him hard. "This ain't some promise you can take back, understand? Once she gets used to an idea, God help us all."

"I ain't someone who goes back on his word."

"You've got no inkling how much your sister has to tell you."

"I can take it." David suddenly ages a few years.

LeeRoy is cornered. "You've got to stay low. Where I put you, you've got to stick. Hear me?" The kid nods and nods. "If you're sure then I think you'd better buckle up."

Following Jack the hemp man's direction, LeeRoy drives out to US 60 and then takes back roads until he sees an old Marlboro billboard. He's concentrating so hard there's no time for radio or cassettes or nothing. Turns right onto a bumpy, pitch-black dirt lane and goes a good ten miles before a huge circle of headlights glares up in the middle of a dirt field. The boy is bouncing up and down. LeeRoy has to admit, his own ramped-up heart is making it uncomfortable to breathe.

Red joins the circle, lights left on. In the center is a cob-bled-together arena just big enough for a cowboy and his ride. Nothing but saddle bronc tonight.

He decides to put on his chaps, untangling the fringes. It's high time he earns his grandpop's buckle. The hat takes time to get just right. Everyone has on a cowboy hat at midnight. He feels so good he gives David's shoulder a squeeze. Maybe it's not a bad idea to play hero to H's little brother.

Right as they walk off, he hears something creaking from his truck. The tailgate opens. He feels sick, thinking a ghost is messing with Red. First comes dusty-brown canvas shoes with a circle of yellow, then ill-fitting pants, then long sleeves, then out pops H.

LeeRoy's throat clogs; his heart drops to his toes.

"Ai gô," she announces all casual, like everyone rides to a midnight rodeo as a stowaway.

When she's bouncy, that's when he worries most. "What the hell is wrong with the both of you?"

She turns to the boy, whose eyes are the size of golf balls, and says a long something in Vietnamese, finishing with "é-vờ-ri đây lân-chờ." LeeRoy has to repeat "every day lunch" for the boy's sake, emphasizing there's no getting out of a story a day now.

David deflates. LeeRoy eyes her hard. "Why are you here?"

129

"Bờ-ró-đờ gô, Ai gô."

LeeRoy groans.

David sighs, "Oh man."

But this ain't the time to sort out the mess. In the lit arena, a rider clings to a revved-up bronc, most probably an arm jerker. There's no chute, just a pickup man holding on to the halter as best he can before letting go and getting out of the way. The bronc bucks hind legs, the crowd starts chanting, "one, two," the bronc thrashes, "three, four," the rider starts to grab the saddle, but saves himself. Another no-pattern buck, "five . . ." The rider goes flying and thumps the dirt on his chest. The crowd gives a half-hearted cheer.

The rider doesn't get anything for that ride. The rule is a cowboy has got to stay on eight seconds like the professionals to win a prize. Onlookers, though, are free to gamble on when he might fall off. They can bet on anything as long as they can find someone to bet with.

All three of them run toward the action. H is in the middle, but the boy moves so LeeRoy is in the middle. David won't stand by his sister, how's he supposed to sit through their lunch talks? But LeeRoy doesn't care. Another rider is raring to go. Then another. Bodies fly every which way like that prank where squiggly worms pop out of cans. No one talks. Everybody is counting.

At break, LeeRoy has in mind only one destination: the

sign-up line. He's feeling strong. His grandpop's buckle is going to look right smart on his shriveled-up waistline.

But the man at the gate flicks away LeeRoy's five bucks.

LeeRoy narrows his eyes. "Why cain't I ride?"

"We don't cater to no shiny cowboys." The man about spits. "You can get hurt bad out here. Go play rodeo somewhere else."

H glares at the man, which makes LeeRoy feel a little better, then she ruins it by tugging on his sleeve. "Gô hôm." David shakes his head so hard it might pop off, his eyes puppy-dog–like and begging LeeRoy to stay.

"Go home?" LeeRoy is stumped. "We've barely started poking around."

He walks ahead, for sure H is glaring at the both of them. He ignores her. If the kid's smart, he would too.

They end up near two hired hands. Come to think of it, all the cowboys here look like workers in bad need of showers. Does no one have pride anymore? Bruce Ford flatters the cowboy image wherever he goes.

LeeRoy can't help but talk about his rejection. "I just want to honor my grandpop, even if it ain't bareback, you get me?"

"'Course you did. What that man did was uncalled-for, it truly was," the one with a beard says.

The other spits snuff. "If you're hankering for a ride, I got somethin'."

"For real?"

H chooses this moment to bug LeeRoy. "NÔ, nô," she says, pinching his arm hard.

LeeRoy swats at her. "Shooo."

The cowboys walk behind the parked trucks to where it's much darker. All three follow.

A horse in a trailer. LeeRoy whistles. The boy slaps his thigh. H shakes her head.

"This buddy here ain't all that ornery, but he's no runaway," one says while the other leads the horse out. "Still got plenty of good bucking in him."

The horse stands still, looking tame as anything, saddled and ready to go.

"How much y'all charging?" LeeRoy barely gets the question out before H stations herself behind him, pushing him away from the horse.

"Du nót ri-eo cao-bồi," she hisses.

"Stop saying that. I AM A REAL COWBOY!" LeeRoy is so mad he feels tingly. "This ain't your business."

One of the men yells out, "That little Chinese girl won't let you ride? Tell her if you stay on for four counts, not even eight, it's on us. If you get bucked, cost you five bucks. If you manage until eight, hell, we'll give you the damn saddle. You would have earned it."

LeeRoy digs in his heels, turns around, and counts in H's

face. "One, two, three, four. Who cain't do that? What if I win the saddle? Something, right? A cowboy needs his saddle more than his horse, bet you don't know that. He can always get another horse, but a good-fittin' saddle broken in just for him, hum . . ."

"Ai em nót Chai-ni-sì!"

LeeRoy should have renamed her STUBBORN. His own foul mood has lifted. He punches her arm. "Of course you're not Chinese. Relax, will ya?"

The men lead the horse to a mound of hay, hold on to it until LeeRoy mounts. He smells beer. They're probably full as a tick. Still he mounts, unstable from being so high up.

Truth is he hasn't been on a horse since taking pony rides as kid. But he has memorized about all the tricks and techniques Bruce Ford preaches. Abs tight, hips back, shoulders square, chin tucked, eyes on the middle front, one hand extended while holding the hack rein centered with the horse and his body, all the while dragging his heels back with toes pointed out as he squeezes his heels as close to his behind as possible.

LeeRoy holds the reins with his right hand and accidentally puts his left on the saddle horn. His stomach lurches. He knows. But it's too late.

Both cowboys are stumbling and laughing as they smack the bronc, calling out, "Whoooo wweeeee."

It happens in seconds. The bronc bucks back legs. LeeRoy flies forward. His crotch slams into the saddle horn that should never ever be on a saddle for bronc riding. He falls. Thousands of searing hot shrapnels scatter in his groin and shoot up his stomach, where muscles contract so hard he throws up just as he hits dirt. He lands on his back but doesn't feel it. All the pain contracts in his gut. Numb everywhere else. He sweats and shakes and vomits some more. Laughter buzzes in his ears.

H's warm palm is on his forehead. She leans toward him, talking in that lilting language so fast and so pretty.

Then her body whips around, hand flashing something from her ankle. He looks up at a knife, at a tight white grip. His body turns to mush and blends into the ground.

Slow Bumpy Ride

Hằng flicks the knife and yells, "Gô."

The men keep laughing. The one not holding the horse comes closer. "What ya got there, darling?"

She knows and hates what's underneath the sneer. She steps between the men and her brother. She needs momentum. It's better if she runs, thrusting the blade into his gut, then twisting it, rather than wait for him to grab her. She didn't have a knife on the island. That was why she had to hide in a cave.

Invisible bites dart underneath skin like poisoned arrows burning, itching, searing neck to toes. Each tiny step another dot, drawing long twisty lines in red.

She pinches her thigh, hard. Desperation always stirs up memories, which for a while have been supplanted by ranch work. Muscle aches have served her well.

She charges.

Someone holds her by the waist, yanks away her knife. She turns fingers into claws, ready to sink nails deep into any flesh. But it's the hemp straw man. Her heart bounces so high she has to open her mouth to take a breath.

He takes her knife, whispers, "They ain't worth your spit, young miss."

To the evil men he yells, "Git. You know what's coming to ya."

They smile. "No hard feelings, Jack. This dumbass was the one who had it coming. Playin' cowboy like he's on his daddy's ranch."

They go away. She sinks to the ground next to Ly-Roi. As pitiful as he looks, she feels sadder for the horse, who can't escape those loud, spit-drool men.

The hemp man squats down. "He'll be all right after a good, cold drink. I'll be back."

He returns her knife. Just in case, she guesses, slipping it inside its sheath.

Her brother sits on Ly-Roi's other side. She signals for his shirt. He hesitates. It looks like a brand-new shirt, crisp and ironed. In boots and a cowboy hat, Linh looks like the man he'll be one day.

The crowd continues to count. She signals for the shirt

again, acting out how she'll wash and iron it. Her brother relents and looks down at his friend. The sacrifice is for Ly-Roi, not her. Still, her heart expands. This is the closest she's been face-to-face with Linh in a long, long time.

He probably wonders why she does not offer her own long-sleeve. But never could she expose her skin, even on the most moonless inky night. No one can ever see the many loopy lines in red.

Hằng wipes Ly-Roi's mouth. The man returns, holding a drink with ice. He shakes Ly-Roi awake and makes him sip plenty to replenish what has soaked a shirt.

Helpers come and place Ly-Roi on a plank of wood, which is slid into his truck bed on a mat already unfolded. How he groans. Hằng and her brother crawl in too, squeezed among boxes and dirty clothes and sour sweat. She fumbles for her bag with straps, hidden there from her secret ride earlier.

The man drives. His friend follows in another truck.

Ly-Roi lies in the middle, with Hằng leaning on one side, her brother the other. A slow, bouncy ride. Dark. A breeze from side windows. If dozens more bodies are crammed here and the vomit and sweat a hundred times worse and if they envision drumsticks and rice bowls in the stars and if salty sea water burns their sores and teases their thirst, they would all be inside a boat together.

She reaches into her bag for a last nub of ginger, saved for this kind of emergency. The other ginger pieces should be growing plump and wide in her garden box, among celery and tomatoes and bell peppers and leafy greens. She gnaws. Dry, hard flakes bloom against saliva, awakening the fire of the tropics. The drier the nub, the more potent when soaked.

Linh breathes so close by. The heat of him ricochets against Ly-Roi's skin then against hers. Moonbeams sliver in. Her brother's eyes are on hers. These eyes once implored her to tell him stories, to get him to school, to cut open a fruit, any fruit at all. He should be the first to hear the truth.

"It was my fault. I was wrong to pretend we were orphans. I never meant for you to come here alone, do you believe me? Remember when we rode on the xe lam, so crowded you sat on my lap with your chubby legs dangling and a lady held a duck next to us and you asked if the duck likes mini-bus rides, remember? I should not have lured you to the airport promising a horse in a new land. How you laughed and bucked. I should not have told you we would see Bà and our father and our mother over there.

"Remember what you sang so the duck wouldn't feel bus sick? 'Kìa con bướm vàng, kìa con bướm vàng,' remember?

"In the chaos no one checked for papers. I didn't know they would only want orphans three or younger. You were five, but still baby-faced enough to pass.

"All the way home I arranged words to confess that I

accidentally gave you away. Bà met me at the door. I babbled
about a man, a plane, and Bà concluded you'd been kidnapped.

"Each day we plotted to retrieve you. I didn't know it would
take so long. I didn't calculate how you would have grown. You
look glossy and meaty. You have been well watched. Do you for-
give me? I am so sorry, my little one. I yearned to see a horse. I
wanted you to, too. Do you forgive me?

"Do you forgive me?"

Ly-Roi stirs, whispers, "He might not understand you. He
was so little then."

Hằng's stomach convulses. She has called upon every nerve
to tell her brother the entire story. But she was confessing into
nothingness. Why had she assumed Linh would still understand a language from the very beginning of his being? Of
course he would forget. She must stop thinking of him as then.
Or she'll keep getting him wrong.

"Du ân-đờ-sì-ten mi?" she asks her brother, in a language
where she's the baby talker and he's the accomplished speaker.
She had witnessed his first word: Bà.

Ly-Roi whispers, taking tiny breaths. "David, you understand her?"

The boy, her boy, shakes his head.

She asks Ly-Roi to tell her brother she's very sorry. Linh
doesn't respond. Is it her imagination or does he look sad?

It's been a long night. She lies down on one side of Ly-Roi, her brother on the other. Upper arms touch. She gnaws on desiccated ginger and remembers that when sick, people sing. On the boat, someone was always humming even after no one could manage a full-throated song. She sings.

> *Kìa con bướm vàng, kìa con bướm vàng*
> *Xòe đôi cánh, xòe đôi cánh*
> *Tung cánh bay lên thăm trời, tung cánh bay lên thăm*
>   *trời*
> *Em ngồi xem, em ngồi xem.*

Her brother's once-favorite song. She sings again and again about a butterfly, in hopes her brother might join her. He does not. She sings on the slow, long ride home, and at some point she hums. It feels just as good to hum.

It could be because she's sleepy, but she thinks her brother is humming too.

She hums and Ly-Roi squeezes her hand, once.

The Good, the Bad, the Ugly

Breakfast used to be LeeRoy's favorite part of the day. Lately though his stomach keeps flip-flopping like a politician, wrecking his appetite.

It's not because he's still black and blue down there, even though the soreness did go away. At least he no longer walks like he's trying to get around muck.

And it's not because of the mounds of bullshit work Mr. Morgan has dreamed up to punish all three of them. C'mon, who can resist a midnight rodeo? But Mr. Morgan has been enraged, hissing that fake rodeo folks are "more crooked than a dog's hind legs."

H loved the saying, made him write it down. Giddy, she drew a dog with crooked legs and jotted down each syllable in a way that only she understands. LeeRoy never knows what's going to set her off as far as happy or angry.

If Mr. Morgan was already cranky on a daily basis, the last few he's been downright mean. Day one after the rodeo, when LeeRoy was barely limping, he made them polish the windmill. Nobody can see or would care about shiny nuts and bolts on a windmill. But good God Almighty, polish them they did. Pain zipped through every nerve when LeeRoy climbed each step of the ladder. Of course he was stuck with the highest task, mopping the blades.

Then the Meanie had them scrub all eleven troughs with vinegar and baking soda. The horses flared their nostrils and refused to drink until the stink evaporated. Next they set traps for prairie dogs, catching not a one. The damn dogs were probably laughing at them.

David has been enduring his share like a grown-up. Bet he'll think twice before sneaking off to a midnight anything.

The pain and punishment, though, don't account for LeeRoy feeling poorly. It's H. Gets worse every time he glances at her. She's changed since rodeo night from an annoying, grumpy sidekick to an annoying, grumpy girl. By his own admission he did reach out and squeeze her hand in the back of the truck. At the time, it was a gesture of solidarity, as they were both plum worn out. He didn't know one dad-gum squeeze would leave him feeling like he swallowed cobwebs.

He's got no inkling what to do about it. The last piece of bacon, he puts on her plate.

"Nô." She sours up her face. David snatches it up.

"You are ungrateful, you know that, H?" LeeRoy is surprised how mad he sounds. But every little thing she does, or he does for her, somehow gets magnified from a pea to a mountain these days.

"Du lao-đờ."

Why is *she* not feeling hesitant and hopeful and shy and overwhelmed? Maybe she is. That's the part that gets him. He's got no idea if her gut does a hundred little cartwheels when she looks at him.

"Yeah? You're louder." LeeRoy doesn't know why he keeps at it. "And it's 'You ARE loud.' Say your 'be' verbs."

That gets him a glare on par with bright beams. "Du ân-đờ-sì-ten mi?"

"Yeah, I understand you, but that's not the point."

"Nót nét-sì-xe-ri," she grumbles.

"Yes, necessary." LeeRoy could argue a whole lot more, but he's relieved The Tormentor has walked in.

"Grab lunch. Come out," Mr. Morgan barks.

He, H, and David jump at leftovers. No one wants to be caught without grub, not with the kind of hell their bodies are under. At lunch Mr. Morgan usually gives them minutes before the meal is done for. Still, H has been trying in between chews to enunciate each word to talk to her brother. Her English does take getting used to, with all them extra hisses. But the poor kid has done nothing more than stare at his biscuits and sausages.

Outside four horses stand saddled and ready. There's Thea, Linh the Horse (can't say just Linh, according to H), Rocket, and Gracie. The last two are old-time trail horses. No matter who's riding them, they go to the same spot, at the same pace, then turn back to the stable. Frankie the donkey stands hooked to a wagon packed with tools. Not a good sign.

LeeRoy looks down at his still-nursing private part and feels dizzy. H's face is white.

"Sir, I'm in no condition to . . ."

Mr. Morgan cuts in, "Y'all will ride."

David mounts just fine. H hesitates, as if thinking of some excuse. Mr. Morgan stares her down. Left foot in the stirrup, swings her right leg over, she's on Rocket. Mr. Morgan adjusts her stirrups.

She looks like someone who's been thrust into midair and left there. The gigantic hat doesn't help her acquire the cowgirl look, not one bit. At least LeeRoy has found a frayed cowboy hat, which he's starting to prefer to his own.

LeeRoy clambers on Gracie. Owww. He doesn't cry out though, not wanting more gawking at his private business. He sees all of them glancing down there every now and then, wondering plenty, but thank the Lord no one has asked about it.

Of all the idiotic things this summer, he's sickened that H was there to witness the worst of it. But it was nice to have her near, her upper arm against his.

There was that one time when David insisted that the vet examine LeeRoy after checking on Linh the Horse.

"I haven't got the goods of a horse," LeeRoy tried to reason. "That there vet cain't do a thing for me."

The vet agreed right away. But David nagged until they both went into an empty stall, turned their backs, and the vet pretended to have a look. LeeRoy would have traded a broken arm, or even shattered ribs. He's starting to feel like Grandpop has got nothing on him.

Once everyone has mounted, they're off. Mr. Morgan's leading, H bouncing behind, then LeeRoy, equally bouncy, and finally David, shouting instructions.

"Y'all gotta post on a long trot, easier on a horse's back, even in Western, now lift, get in rhythm with your horse, y'all gotta raise your bottoms and hips to every bump, up, down, up, down. Tighten your entire legs, roll just a little forward on your inner thighs. Y'all gotta not grip with your heels or the horse will canter. One two, one two."

LeeRoy hisses at him, "Will you hush?"

Both his and H's bee-hinds keep bobbing. His tailbone, likely hers too, is making acquaintance with the saddle like they're best buds. But he gripes in silence, thinking of count-less cowboys who endured a whole lot more out on the trail.

H keeps tilting to the right and LeeRoy's afraid she'll bounce right off.

"H, sit up straight."

"Du ri-eo cao-bồi? Du đu nót nô," she shoots back.

"I'm done telling you I'm a real cowboy, and I know plenty, believe you me, I know."

That does it. The hell with her, no more Mr. Nice Guy. He tries to giddy up Gracie, but the old trail horse can't be both-ered. This cowboy life, it asks an awful lot from a man.

After a long while, Mr. Morgan stops next to a big mes-quite, ties a long red strip of cloth on the highest branch. "What I mark, y'all will yank out, root and all. Don't damage the trunk. I carve every bit."

Three little sentences and LeeRoy's back is already scream-ing. A mesquite is not a tree any right-minded human should be getting near, much less wrestle out of the ground, not with them gnarly pokey branches and roots that can crawl two hun-dred feet underground.

LeeRoy has to ask, "How do you figure we'll get it out?"

"Think on that amongst yourselves."

Thea walks on; the other horses follow. LeeRoy doesn't bother to ask how many more trees Mr. Morgan aims to mark in his vast sixty acres. The three of them likely will grow old before they get ahold of the first one.

Thea finally stops. So do the others. Before them, the earth opens up and sinks down into a canyon glowing in the morning sun in layers of gray, yellow, pink, purple, red, and brown. They don't call it a Spanish skirt for nothing. Both he and H gasp.

"Wow," he says.

"Tut, tut, tut, tut, tut," she adds, clicking her tongue, shaking her head. That must also mean "wow" from the delight on her face.

Mr. Morgan is surprised. "Y'all haven't seen the Grand Canyon of Texas?"

Of course not, LeeRoy almost shouts, you haven't exactly allowed time for touristing. But why ruin this moment? Who would have guessed that his land butts into the eye-popping Palo Duro Canyon?

Mr. Morgan points to a tall mesquite and throws LeeRoy a red strip.

"Hang it high," he says.

LeeRoy pipes up. *"Hang 'Em High."*

Mr. Morgan actually smiles. "Fine picture show."

H whips her head toward LeeRoy. Her narrowed eyes scorching. "Hằng, nót Hang," she spits.

"No one is bothering with your name." It's just like her to ruin Mr. Morgan's one good mood. "We're talking here about a Clint Eastwood Western."

She brightens. "Clin Ít-gút? *Đờ Gút, đờ Bét, đờ Ấc-ly.*"

Mr. Morgan smiles again. "You know *The Good, the Bad, and the Ugly*? An even better show."

It amazes LeeRoy what H has jammed up in her brain. "That theme song, once you hear it, you never forget it, Ah-Ah-Ah-Ah Wah Wah Wah." LeeRoy whistles the tune for good measure.

H goes back to scowling. "Nô, O-Ó-O-Ò Hoa Hoa Hoa." She whistles too, which sounds closer to the real thing. She repeats, "O-Ó-O-Ò Hoa Hoa Hoa."

LeeRoy's irritated. Nobody messes with the best soundtrack ever made. "It's Ah-Ah-Ah-Ah Wah Wah Wah, gunfire, gunfire."

H glares. "Ai nô *Đờ Gút, đờ Bét, đờ Ấc-ly*. Mú-vì mai phá-đờ lớp. O-Ó-O-Ò Hoa Hoa Hoa. Lai rút-sì-tờ in mó-ninh."

"No way no how it sounds like a rooster!" LeeRoy's got a pretty good glare himself.

But she won't quit. "Do soong lai-kờ bấy-bì cờ-rai-inh."

"Wah-Wah-Wah is not a baby crying," he about screams. "You're the baby."

"Du bích-gờ bấy-bì."

She dares to mock him as the bigger baby. LeeRoy is ramping up a cutting comeback when Mr. Morgan yells, "Cut it out!" The boss man truly has stopped smiling. "What's eating at y'all has got nothing to do with a picture song. Git to work."

LeeRoy turns red and looks down, just for a minute. In that little time Thea has trotted off. For some punishing reason, the other three horses stay put. The boy has slipped down and is flipping through shovels, spades, saws, gloves, cotton arm wraps. The wagon also holds three huge jugs of water. Meaning it's going to be a long, long day under the terrorizing sun.

LeeRoy gets down and ties up Gracie. Rocket, though, turns right around and heads off with H. The sight plays out like a joke: a girl dressed up as a hired hand, heading to the beach on horseback, flaunting a gigantic sun hat. Rocket gets up to a trot. H bounces along, leaning way to the right. LeeRoy calls for her to even up, to pull at the reins, but what's the use?

David says, "It's better she goes."

"You might be right about that."

LeeRoy plays along to cover up a pinch of longing as he watches her go. Then he stares at a much bigger predicament—the mesquite that's got to somehow come clean out of the ground.

Memories on the Tongue

The lumbering brown giant walks into the stable, snorts for Hằng to get off. She would have done so without prompting.

"Never again," she grumbles. *"Never will I sit so high from earth."*

Hằng knows to remove the saddle and pad, then walk the horse just long enough to dry slabs of muscle. She tries to stay ahead of its head, ahead of gigantic rubbery nostrils nubbing for treats in her neck, armpit, shirt pocket. Finding nothing, it snorts at her and turns away. Her brother has managed to spoil all the horses, not just his beloved one.

As she walks toward the garden her legs curve out and re-meet as if she's still straddling a horse. Finally she understands why movie cowboys lumber around like they're holding a barrel between their legs.

She goes toward the task she understands well, cantaloupes. It's odd that their soil still doesn't need watering, but her one plot does. Maybe vegetables drink a lot more. She eats baby leaves on everything but the towering tomatoes. If not for this plot of greens, she's certain her insides would have clogged up, protesting the mounds of meat constantly on the table. After harvest she yearns to sauté mature greens with oil and garlic. But that will require the bravery to ask Ông Mó-gân for the use of his pan and stove. It might be calmer to keep devouring everything raw.

Long, thin leaves smelling and tasting of ginger have reached arm's length. Underneath the soil, the world's best medicine is growing, thrilling her as she throws feed to the chickens.

Chores done, Hằng waits on the porch for Ông Mó-gân. But he's probably spying on the boys. In her pocket sits the little notebook heavy with stories, now at 184, of which her brother has heard three. For each telling, she calculates out five sentences. It torments her brain, this squeezing of English.

Every sentence forces her to contemplate subject-predicate agreement, matching tenses (remembering the tense is determined by the first word in a verb phrase), transitive verbs needing a direct object, or intransitive verbs requiring none, or irregular verbs that can't add -ed for past tense, then the pronoun must match the noun, then ridiculous articles "a, an, the" (if dismissed the meaning would remain unaltered), dangling modifiers, gerunds that can be subjects or objects, then parts of speech that require dizzying costume changes. After all that, she must pronounce the whole scheme and hope her brother can understand.

Fifteen blood-pricking sentences so far. In return her brother has kept silent while staring at his round bread and matching salty round meat. Such brutal throat-scratching food.

From the list she practices a story about bedtime, calculating each grammar rule as if doing mental math. Yet the first attempt always comes out awkward.

"Bà and I talk you night every before sleeps."

No, should be "talked." There's an annoying little word that must tag along with the verb: "of." They spoke more than one night, so "nights." She remembers now, in English the adjective is positioned before the noun, thus "every night," with the adjective determining the singular form. Should "sleep" be plural? No, sleep is an idea, like love, no *s*.

So many decisions in a single simple sentence. Exhausting, this elaborate dance of words. Her pencil wanders, and she's surprised to finish with a word tree—a trick her father taught her to tame English, to rip open its core and see every vein.

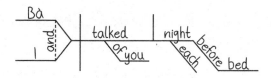

She arranges four more trees about bedtime. The words fly themselves into the right slots, leaving time to turn toward the question she longs to ask.

In such a tree her desperation becomes affirmative, obliterating the question mark. A perfect sentence, concise and hopeful. If only she could squeeze her brother into a word tree. If not that, then she'll do what's possible—she'll share the trees with him.

Next on the story list is his favorite fruit, *trái măng cụt.* Instead of a word tree, it would be easier still to feather brush a purple-black circular shell topped with a four-leaf star. She pencil-dusts an image where the upper half of the fruit is sliced off to reveal six bright white segments cuddled inside a brown-pink core. When they were in season, Bà used to exchange vitamin C tablets for baskets of purple-black balls.

A tree thick with leathery leaves and dark bark, used to ease stomach cramps. Slimy black seeds. A white segment between baby teeth. Inside penciled images, she imagines colors glowing raw and deep. A smell floral, ripe, fleeting like the passing of a jasmine peddler at dawn. A taste soft, slightly acidic, smoothly sweet. So real she almost licks the page. A puddle pools in her mouth.

Linh will remember. Memories will return on his tongue.

She pockets the notebook and runs toward her brother, only to realize he's kilometers away. But never again a horse for her. Perhaps she can drive Red. Ly-Roi will have to forgive her. Near the truck she sees a bicycle, leaning, rusting, against the side of an old barn.

Pushy Uncle

As soon as LeeRoy sees Hằng wobble back to work, he pinches his lips to hush. It's her business if she aims to man-handle a rusty, creaky bicycle. He might not be the world's best cowboy, but he knows to pick an old trail horse over a pile of junk that requires muscle work.

All afternoon they keep at the mesquite. The roots ain't budging. When they run out of water, LeeRoy barely calls out, "Quitting time," before they all throw down their shovels.

Close to the house, LeeRoy and H stop short seeing a low-riding sports car. Last time her uncle showed up he was pushy with getting her to sign this, agree to that. Only David is innocent enough to keep trotting.

The uncle comes running toward the boy. "Linh, I have great news."

The horse looks up while the boy keeps his eyes on the stable. The uncle looks hurt. LeeRoy can't help it. He always has to make everybody feel better. "Hey there, Uncle. David rides past me all the time. Did you happen to snatch up any more of them pastries?"

Ignoring LeeRoy, the man heads straight to his niece and talks fast and low in their language. Hằng looks like she wants to get away.

LeeRoy slips down and tries to distract the uncle. Figuring Hằng will remember the gesture the next time she decides to sass him.

"Settle something for us, will ya? *The Good, the Bad, and the Ugly,* does it go Ah-Ah-Ah-Ah Wah Wah Wah, gunfire, gunfire, or like this." He points to Hằng.

She jumps right in. "O-Ó-O-Ò Hoa Hoa Hoa."

LeeRoy insists, "Which is it? I'm right, right?"

The uncle pulls out a smile that is too sly for LeeRoy's peace of mind. "Here's the deal, whoever I pick has to do me one tiny favor, got it?" He repeats the instructions in Vietnamese.

Nods all around.

"Everybody hears O-Ó-O-Ò Hoa Hoa Hoa," the uncle decides, then grips Hằng's elbow to escort her to his car.

"Y'all cheated," LeeRoy yells. By then, those two are arguing. Hằng refuses to get in, pushes back a piece of paper he's pressing on her.

"You show him, H."

They look up and actually shush him. Walking inside, Lee-Roy gets in the last word. "Fine, it's not like I'm dying for y'all's company."

Truth to Tell

Chú Quốc attempts a stern face. *"You will sign."*

Hằng feels no threat. *"I must read it slowly."*

He softens, as if remembering to act like a parent. He asks if Ly-Roi is really gone before pulling out a bag. *"Not paté chaud, but I think you like it better."*

He hands Hằng something wrapped in white paper. She smiles before opening, nostrils flaring. There's no mistaking the mix of crispy baguette, seasoned pork, pickled carrot along with daikon, and zingy cilantro, the last three ingredients added just before eating to avoid sogging the bread. She has not known she has been longing for bánh mì until the first bite.

"Keep chewing, sign here and here."

He seems nervous.

Hằng's cheeks puff out. *"I must read it."*

"Skim it, all accurate. You read English?"

She gives him a look that quiets him as she finishes her sandwich. Reading English sinks into her as easily as breathing. Pronouncing such an illogical language, though, prickles her every pore.

She reads:

Two people, a Vietnamese lady and an American man, came to our school and told us to go home and get one sibling, the younger the better. Then on several mini buses they drove us to the airport. There, they separated us by age. I thought we were to perform a song for someone important, or that each student group might receive prizes for being outstanding. Then I realized we were all labeled orphans. I ran to find my brother. An American man was carrying him up a plane ladder. I lunged for my brother, but another American held me back. I screamed. My brother saw me and struggled to get down. He too screamed as he disappeared inside the plane. How he cried for me. The door shut. I was dragged back inside the airport where I watched the airplane shrink in the sky.

Hằng looks confused. *"Bà told you?"*

"How else would I know?" Chú Quốc tries to smile, to be neutral, but Hằng knows he has embellished here and there to build more pathos for the judge.

"Not accurate, no one came to the school to get us."

"How did you get to the airport?"

Hằng opens her mouth. No words escape. Her face contorts.

"You don't have to remember." Her uncle softens his voice. *"The letter does it."*

But she shakes her head and folds the letter, putting it back in its envelope. *"I have a truth to tell."*

Chú Quốc wrinkles his brows, calculating something. *"Will it help get Linh back?"*

"No."

Her uncle bites his lip. *"Tell me something else for now, something happy, something you want everyone to know."*

Skin Peeling Off Bones

"*Father never learned about Linh. Bà always said Father was spared a knotted gut, and that at times not knowing is life's best gift. She wasn't allowed such blindness. In the days right before the war ended, Bà was either bribing someone to retrieve Father's body or pleading with someone else to trace Linh's fate.*

"*We learned nothing more of Linh, but luck aligned for finding Father. His body was brought to the back door wrapped in two rice sacks. Bà spent the rest of her gold burying him in a cemetery squeezed tight with soldiers. All on the losing side. Three years later the Communists announced the land would be converted to a memorial for their soldiers. Bodies not moved would rest for eternity beneath cement, beneath footsteps.*

"*Using a minor portion of the money you sent, Bà hired boys to dig up Father's grave. I went with her on that moon-bright night when his wooden coffin was opened. Rows and rows of bent backs were already there, lifting leathery bodies up to the ground. We knew to bring two buckets of water. We knew to bring a pillowcase to carry him home.*

"Everyone lit incense. Everyone murmured something to the dead, a communal lullaby that muffled individual cries.

"A kind grandmother, older than Bà would ever become, taught us how to peel blackened skin from bones and wash them spotless in the other bucket. I was not allowed to attend to Father's head, eyeholes sunken, no nose, mouth gaping, teeth large and protruding, cheekbones pointy on his taut face. Bà chanted as she washed the head and brought up to the moonlight a clean skull. Father felt cool and wrinkly and smelled of earth. His skin lifted in batches, like peeling off silk gloves. I placed what was left of Father, his skull, his long bones, his short bones, into the pillowcase. Pouring in the wash water, we returned his hair and skin and teeth and lumps to the coffin, which boys covered again with dirt. All mourners were women and girls and boys. No men. Our men were either dead or imprisoned or hiding.

"We brought Father home and Mother rose from her bed and lit incense. We pried up the tiles under the divan. Beneath the tiles, we scooped out earth with spoons and two pans. Deep enough to fit a large tin can that once held rice grains. Mother mumbled good-bye to his skull, to each long bone, to each short

bone as she arranged them in the can. Bà scattered dried herbs. She closed the lid and we lowered him to the ground and patted dirt around the can. Then we replaced the tiles, crooked and wobbly, covered by the divan. The extra dirt we took months to scatter outside, a few palms at a time. Nothing to cause suspicion.

"No one talked of Father out loud. Late at night, though, I often heard Bà whisper to him about our plans to reunite with Linh, about you in the west, about Mother crying in her bed, about me devouring his old English studies as if each word was a cooked grain to be savored long and deep. She told him she had planned to burn all his books so the authorities would not target us. Yet how I pleaded to keep one magazine with horses and one grammar book with word trees. We hid the books inside a sack, within a wall, behind the ancestral altar, bringing them alive only in flickering candlelight."

Hằng looks up to an uncle convulsing in silence. Odd to witness so much snot and tears and shoulder quakes, all circulating without sound. Why is he crying upon hearing her best story, her happy story?

She's relieved to not have told of her eventual removal from school. Would her uncle have shuddered over that story? What about the Communist quadrant leader who insisted Mother come out and greet him?

The leader happened by every dinnertime, quoting Hồ

Chí Minh while smoking in the living room. Bà was the only one to sit with him. She talked as if he was important, as if she owed him her house and life.

A favorite quote of his was *"Labor is the glory."* The leader was irritated hearing of Mother's weepy weakness. Everyone must work, he shouted. Everyone must be useful to Việt Nam. No parasites. If one can't offer brains, then one can contribute sweat by cleaning streets, unclogging sewers, picking caterpillars from leafy greens. Bà nodded and offered him more wine, telling Hằng in secret she didn't bother to correct the leader because cruel people like him exist on every side, in every war. His side won so he got to be right. If the South had won, no doubt the same cruelty would find targets in those who sided with the North, or those who sided with no one at all. His words were only that, words, and for his ears alone. Thousands of years had proven that, while nodding, listeners plotted ways to go around such inflated words.

Bà did not tell the man that she alone raised her sons by using her hands to grow herbs and her brains to turn the plants into ornaments like bonsai, starting a craze as lucrative as grafting orchids. Nor did Bà explain Mother had studied Ayurveda beauty secrets in India and, by creating lotions and oils, supported her husband through enough English courses for him to qualify as a translator.

Bà always said, *"Chết thì chết, sống thì sống, có nhau." Die we die. Live we live. With each other.* But she died without any family nearby.

Hằng no longer can determine which story is worse than the next. The ugliness on the boat and the island, she knows to keep to herself. But the rest of her many stories, which ones can she tell?

Particularly because of what her uncle's wife had whispered during the one night Hằng was in their house. *"Don't tell people you came by boat. Better yet, don't talk about your old life at all,"* her aunt advised. *"Telling would only bring judgment and pity. Better to smile, lift your head, forget, do everything right. Soon your life will be so perfect you will have no need to remember, much less tell."*

The aunt slipped out of the room before Hằng thought to reply, *"You know nothing."*

She smiles at her collapsed uncle, conveying she can tell a better story, a happier story. But he jumps out of the car. She does too, on her side. Perhaps he would like to walk, perhaps she should pat his arm. The way Bà used to calm her.

Just as Hằng closes her door, her uncle climbs back in and speeds away, probably breaking into full-throated sobs.

She blinks away the twirling dust. The unsigned letter still in her hand.

Swells of Saliva

David just wants to cram down eggs and bacon without fuss. But as soon as LeeRoy and the girl sit, they start in on each other. So boring, a whole summer of them fighting. He wants so bad to shout, "Shut up." With Mama as his mama though, he can't ever say "shut up" out loud. He misses her. Since getting dragged into the big punishment, he's been too tired to say more than "Morning" and "Night."

LeeRoy grumbles while chewing through a whole biscuit, "Red ain't pulling out that devil stump, she's been put upon enough."

The girl bangs down her fork, says something fierce. LeeRoy swears she speaks English, but David makes out only the word "idea."

LeeRoy stabs his grits. "Talk about being stubborn, you make mules seem downright congenial."

She comes right back with something or other, all the while chewing. The three of them eat fast, then grab everything halfway edible and stuff it all in cloths. It's going to be another long, windless, stinking day frying under the sun.

The phone rings. The same man has been calling since screeching out of here yesterday in his burgundy sports car. A sweet ride, but nothing compared to towering over the world on Linh. The phone keeps ringing while they all chew and blink. From his room Mr. Morgan yells, "And?"

LeeRoy picks up and hands it straight to her. She listens a good long while before saying, "No." The phone goes back on the wall.

"C'mon, just sign whatever your uncle wants so we can make an extra hundred bucks and fix up Red and get outta here." LeeRoy looks hopeful.

She shakes her head and chomps on a banana like it's peanut brittle.

A voice of terror hollers from the back, "Git."

They go.

Outside, the girl runs over and climbs into Red. Now Lee-Roy has a turn at head shaking, so hard his mustache might come loose. They go at it as he tries to pull her out of his truck. She talks long and fast.

LeeRoy answers, "You mean it, you'll sign the damn letter and let me mail it to him?"

She nods and mumbles.

"Tonight then." LeeRoy actually smiles before getting in Red.

David knows better than to ride with them. Mama's orders. He follows on Linh. Frankie the donkey comes last, pulling the equipment trailer.

When David catches up at the mesquite stump, they're at it again.

"If you cain't manage a knot, then get out of the way." LeeRoy picks up the girl and sets her aside like a puppy. "I swear to the Almighty, when I get out of this hellhole you will never catch me doing a lick of ranch work ever again."

The girl stomps back to her spot. She throws one end of a rope around the stump and tries a weird loop, all the while grumbling.

LeeRoy sighs. "You're about as pleasant as hugging a rose-bush but I'll go drive, cause Miss Know-It-All here says so."

The truck idea is pretty good thinking, David has to admit. Yesterday they dug and heaved and pulled and yanked, with two horses and a bicycle of all things, but that stump barely budged. It took everything they had to hack away the branches and to saw off the trunk.

LeeRoy loops his end of the rope to a truck trailer hook. He gets in. The engine is loud. Red inches forward. A little more.

The rope is strained, a little more, more. Then a snap right in the middle. Two pieces of rope go flying, one end smacking Red's already wounded side.

"Doggone it, mine is the most punished truck on God's green earth!" LeeRoy gets out, smooths his palm over a slight dent. He turns toward the girl, his eyes trying to be mean. But he can't pull it off. There's no real threat from him no matter what comes out his mouth. "Got any other notion?"

She signals for him to try it again.

So they do it again and again and the stump stays put. They run out of rope and try a chain. Still nothing. They stand around with hats off; the one on the girl is so big and stupid. They wipe sweat from their eyes. Mixed with sunblock, which Mama insisted on, what sneaks into David's eyes stings bad, like poisoned arrows.

LeeRoy smooths down his sweaty horseshoe mustache, which does help him look like a cowboy. "Now what? Back to pulling with two horses and a bicycle? Or do you want us to strap ourselves in and pull too?"

The boy pipes up before they start fistfighting. "Lunch, y'all?" It's not anywhere near lunchtime, but they're hungry. They're always hungry.

David tends to Linh and the donkey first, otherwise they'd whine and shift and stir up a dust cloud. He gives them clumps of grains and molasses, which they love almost as much as the mints, then yucky warm water. "Be good." He crinkles peppermints in his pocket as bribes. They won't be patient for long. David hurries and unties his smooshed pile of lunch. Not caring that the cinnamon bun has sweated into a soggy mess while the biscuit and sausage are now a fatty clump. The bananas have turned swishy brown, but he devours three and saves the peels, which Mr. Morgan always asks after.

It's so hot. The little bit of shade from the equipment trailer eases nothing. Stinging sweat keeps finding David's eyeballs. His hands are blistered and his skin peeling. Muscles ache in places he didn't know he had muscles.

David can't wait for school to start. Two more weeks. Never thought he would be counting down to sixth grade. At least then he'll get flag football during recess. His days will be under a roof. There'll be ice-cold juice at lunch.

Drinking sun-baked water, he knows it's talking time. No way to escape it. He did promise to listen. Soon as chewing stops the girl always comes over, pulling from her pocket a folded sheet of paper.

She talks, saying the same thing LeeRoy has helped him understand for the other four drawings. "Remember? You eat it. You love it." No, he doesn't remember and wishes she would quit talking like it's still true.

Since the first drawing of a round thing with a clover on top and six parts inside, she's gotten ahold of coloring pencils. Today's fruit is oval, faint red with green spears coming out of the peel like crooked fingers. Another sketch shows it's white inside with lots of specks of black seeds. Would people eat the seeds? It seems impossible to spit out every one of them. Saliva gathers in his mouth, something barely sweet with a hint of sour.

"*Trái thanh long*," she says, and nods with eager eyes for David to repeat.

LeeRoy always sticks his nose into the mix. "C'mon kid, you promised to talk. *Try tang lung*, that right?"

David does his part. "*Try tang lung?*"

She's not impressed. She's never impressed. "Nô, nô, *trái thanh long.*"

LeeRoy saves them. "H, give us points for trying. Why do you think I call you H instead of, you know, your name?"

Linh starts fussing and David hops to her, crinkling what's in his pocket. If he plays it right and stays hidden between her and the donkey, the other two might forget about him and busy themselves for a long while with their silly word game. Then he'd be free to brush Linh and soak in the heat and safety in her neck.

Every time Mr. Morgan has been out of sight lately, those

two diagram sentences. David made the mistake of calling them weird drawings when he showed LeeRoy that first note from the girl: "You do forgive me." David never got around to asking forgive her for what. He got distracted on account of LeeRoy pouncing on him. "Not drawings, they're diagrams, it's an art, learned it from my mama, got it?"

They keep at this art even though they fight and holler and shuffle and erase each other's words in the dirt.

LeeRoy calls out today's first challenge. "Getting something done with her is like putting socks on a rooster."

Looking smug and confused all at once, the girl picks up a stick and scribbles.

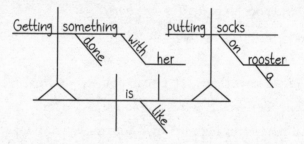

LeeRoy spits, amazed. "How come you know about gerunds as subject and predicate adjective? Except 'like' is all wrong."

He places "like" under "putting."

She switches "like" back and hits LeeRoy's hand with her

stick. He frowns. She frowns, writes out her challenge in a plain sentence: He deserves every stab of thorn.

He narrows his eyes and draws his take:

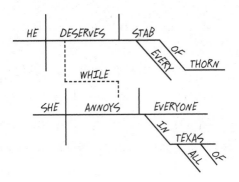

She erases and adds:

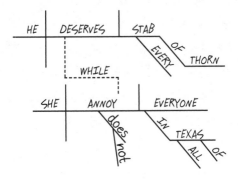

Now they're jostling for position to scratch new words, raising all kinds of dust under the heating-up sun. One minute they seem mad, then they laugh, then they push, then they stamp out more words.

David has to ask, "Do y'all like each other or something?"

He shouldn't have said it. They glare at him, being sure not to look at each other. Just like that, lunch is over. They return to the stump.

Late afternoon Mr. Morgan rides over for an inspection, disappointed as always. Behind his back, David and LeeRoy call him Mr. Meaner Than a Skilletful of Rattlesnakes. It's long, but LeeRoy likes his words. Mr. Meaner couldn't be bothered that the three of them have been stabbed every which way, with them thorns poking right through wraps and jeans and shirts and hats. Their faces never stood a chance. Random dots of blood make them out to have popped pimples they haven't got. At least the day is over.

Mama stands waiting when they get back to the stable. David slips off Linh and runs to hug her, forgetting to act like a grown boy and forgetting that today is her day off. She peers into his face then examines his arms and pulls up his shirt to inspect his punctured stomach and back.

Her brows get wiggly like she's confused and mad, but mostly mad. "I'll be, Mr. Morgan, what in heaven do you have them doing? My son looks like he's been shot through with pellets." She draws him close and smothers his face into her chest, so bony. He has to struggle free to breathe. "You hurt, sugar? It was supposed to be a lesson, not a prison sentence."

The girl keeps staring at him and his mom, like she can't believe something. She'd start to smile then look worried then back to kinda happy then switch to being sad. It gets tiring watching her.

Mr. Morgan looks puzzled too, as if like Mama he's noticing David for the first time in days. He narrows his eyes then pretends to find something fascinating at his feet.

"It's no big deal, Mama." David wants to spill everything, the heat, the thirst, the stump, muscles ground to hamburger meat. But he's no tattle.

LeeRoy jumps in. It does help to have someone so talkative nearby. "Believe you me, if there's a way to uproot that there mesquite, we'd have done it. I'm liable to volunteer to mend fenceposts at this point. A man's got to decide if he'd rather get flesh pounded from his bones or get mutilated wrangling a tree that has no business in Texas. It's almost not worth all them cattle drives if what hitchhiked here are these bloodthirsty suckers."

Mama keeps glaring at Mr. Morgan. "I'm taking a vacation day tomorrow. David and I will have a high old time, won't we, sweetie?" David nods until he's lightheaded.

She turns to LeeRoy. "You've got to dynamite the roots out."

LeeRoy's mouth falls open. "How does a cowboy go about getting dynamites around here?"

"Never mind that." Mr. Morgan speaks up, still avoiding Mama. "Y'all have tomorrow off. Get clean for supper."

Fearing Mr. Morgan might take back his promise, David runs home, LeeRoy runs to Red, and the girl runs inside.

David is allowed to shower so fast he comes to supper still grimy. He eats a whole chicken pot pie plus four chocolate-chip cookies with ice cream and downs two glasses of buttermilk, as if today's his birthday. Mama even said he can sleep late, then spend all day with Linh, who hasn't had her hooves picked all week. He plans on riding in the opposite direction of the mesquite stump and hunting for grass still green.

Mama comes into his room, picks up the girl's newest drawing on the dresser. She sees the others taped on the wall next to a map of the world. "Want to tell me?"

"Nothing to tell. She says I remember, but I don't." He tapes up the red fruit with green fingers.

"You okay being around her?"

He shrugs. "Not that long until school starts. Then she'll be gone." Even as he says it, he's not sure how he feels about it.

Mama traces the latest fruit, sighing. "It's a wonder what's out there I haven't a clue about."

As David watches her finger move along penciled lines, his tongue swells with saliva. Bunches of it have been sloshing on his tongue whenever he stares at the drawings, but he hasn't admitted it out loud. The sweetest one might be the hairy red balls, so sugary they probably bring on a stomachache. The bigger balls with tops like clover could be sweet and sour, creamy white. The tannish-brown bunch might have a quicker sweetness, fleshy, each with a shiny round black seed like an eyeball. Today's fruit is the size of a potato, maybe watery, and the many black specks should crunch like popping tiny pockets of air.

Mama kisses him goodnight, still looking worried as she watches him brush his teeth. In bed something rises above the mint toothpaste, something floral and light and sweet and fresh, deep inside each taste bud. He swallows and tries to get rid of the taste, which grows all the sweeter.

Real Deal

LeeRoy drives off before daybreak, trampling on any chance of H or David tagging along. Yet it's been so long since he got himself to himself, he doesn't quite know how to go about his day off. He's got to find a rodeo. Then the hours should plump up by themselves.

Tapping on the steering wheel feels good. When rap comes on, he fiddles with the volume until the beat stampedes his voice.

We got hum hum hum, *we got* hum hum *in our heart*
A lot hum hum *we do, you can call* hum hum.

He rewinds but still can't remember the lyrics H had made out clear as day. That girl is full of surprises, most of them bad, but sometimes, he has to admit she is a wonder.

Window down, LeeRoy soaks in the still bearable morning air. The brown land expands so deep he feels like a tiny bug trudging through an empty dirt lot. He can't help but see muscle aches in every cow, every horse, every bush, every blade of parched grass. The sight of a mesquite starts him shivering.

Still, he can't quell his pining for open land or a bucking bronc. Everyone, he figures, has longings that won't fade even when clobbered by cold, brutal facts. Just has to figure out how to fit here after forsaking the life of a ranch hand/cowboy. These folks never seem to sit down or eat snacks or read for fun or even watch TV. He could deal with the loss of all that, but it's the physical pain, the bone-gnawing, muscle-mincing pain that has him staring into his shortcomings.

But first thing, a genuine breakfast. Then he'll see about spending hours among cowboys and broncs. So what if it's looking like he won't see his idol anytime soon. He'll be among Bruce Ford's kind. That'll do for now.

We got rhymes on our mind, we got rockin' in our heart
A lot of things we do, you can call it art
We're bad, we're slick, we're doing it hip
We're gonna rock this record and don't you forget.

Finally, these four stubborn lines. Up ahead, a sign for a country diner calls out to him. It's shaping up to be a fine day.

After two stacks of pancakes, which he vows never again to be deprived of, thick slices of ham, whose existence Mr. Morgan ignores, and half an apple pie, which he truly deserves, LeeRoy finally feels sated as a pig in mud. He chuckles and can't figure out why folks here don't let loose these sayings as often as he does. What's the point of inheriting bucketfuls of colorful language if you're not gunning to use it at every turn? For his part, he aims to show off every idiom he ever memorized.

Two cowboys reach the cash register when he does. LeeRoy tips his hat, relieved to have worn work clothes. It doesn't pay to stick out like a citified boy trying out a rough life. He's learning.

"Howdy, y'all happen to know of a rodeo today in these parts?" LeeRoy controls the urge to smile. Cowboys don't go for wasted words or smiles.

One man answers, "Not a whole lot right now. But there's one off 60 toward Tampa, little more than an hour if you drive right. Go on Farm Road 750 and turn left at the Justin sign and keep going and you'll run smack into it. Nothing fancy, but it'll have a little of everything."

LeeRoy nods. "Much obliged."

"You take care." The other man nods.

Walking to Red, LeeRoy has to look down to hide a grin. Now that was a pleasant exchange. H should be here to witness that these real deals thought he was the real deal. So there goes her nagging about whether he's a real cowboy.

After all, he's got himself sorted out on a horse and now has cheekbones almost as pointy as H's. There's so much room in his old jeans he had to cinch up his belt to the tightest notch. Muscles pop out of nowhere, and if pressured, he can take care of himself in any arm-wrestling match. Never thought he'd get to be an outdoorsy he-man, having been raised by pale, fleshy, liberal academics. Not to be vain, but he wonders if H has noticed he doesn't look half bad.

A rodeo does pop up after a while. A legit-looking and legit-smelling one at that. Hay and shit hang in the air. It's crowded for an out-of-nowhere little thing. Dozens of pickups, all better off than poor Red. LeeRoy pets the dents in his truck, whispering, "Soon, you'll get fixed up soon enough."

Kids are calf roping out in the arena. H would get a kick out of that, maybe thinking her little brother can have at it. But it's harder than it looks. The proof is in the wrist. Swinging a rope counterclockwise above your head, you've got to aim for the back of the running calf's head. Catch any other body part and you've done trash in the loop, affecting your time. Once caught, you've got to jump off your horse and throw down the calf and quickly do two wraps and a hooey with piggin' string. Then you jerk up your hands to stop the clock. If the calf escapes before six seconds, you're a goner. LeeRoy imagines plenty of kids and grown-ups have outright cried in front of God and all. And then there's the consideration of the poor calf getting yanked and slammed. Never mind, H no doubt would protest her brother taking part.

The announcer boasts next up bareback riders will compete for one hundred dollars. Puny compared to what Bruce Ford must be pocketing, but everyone's got to start somewhere. LeeRoy has time to wander over to the concession stands, hoping to see his favorite. Yes sir, there it is in its golden crispy sweet glory. Since he was a boy, he's had a weakness for funnel cakes. They're just fried dough dusted with powdered sugar. So basically a warm doughnut, yet a thousand times better than a doughnut. He buys two.

Out of nowhere a girl in a pink cowgirl hat smiles at him. "You're a hungry fella, aren't ya?"

LeeRoy feels his throat tightening. It's not every day a pretty girl talks to him. They think he's nice and all, and usually get him to help them with math during lunch, but this one doesn't seem to be needing anything.

"Me?"

"See anyone else carrying two of those?" She lifts her hat and fluffs long brown hair, where the ends bounce in looped curls. Just like that, LeeRoy feels the damn thing rising in his crotch. Dadgum it, it's got a mind of its own, announcing itself for no reason at all in the middle of chemistry, math, English. Of course that was when he got called to the chalkboard. Needless to say, he refused to go.

He thinks about trash, about maggots, about decapitated squirrels. It eases down. He looks at the sweet offering in his hands and feels sick.

The girl puts her hat back on. Mercy, LeeRoy thinks. He holds out both funnel cakes. "You, uh, want one?"

She seems genuinely confused. "You think I would eat that? Go ahead, I ain't got your muscles to burn it off."

LeeRoy is pretty sure she's flirting with him. No girl has ever mentioned his muscles before. He did kiss Ashley Stevenson last year because everyone else seemed to have done much much more. They both closed eyes, puckered lips, twirled tongues. But he felt nothing other than lots of teeth. He admits he's really behind in the boy/girl department, but he ought to have felt something. They kissed behind her house then he biked home instead of going inside like she wanted him to. It was a lonesome ride.

The cowgirl touches his arm, shakes him a little. "You don't talk much, do you?"

"I, uh, I talk." LeeRoy wishes he hadn't felt her soft hand on his skin. Damn it if the nuisance isn't at full alert. He stares at the funnel cakes, where pools of grease spread wider and wider. He thinks of flattened toads drying by the side of the road.

Right then a legit cowboy in a red bandanna walks up behind the girl and hugs her waist. "What you talking to this jackass for? Come on, I'm about up."

They run off. LeeRoy feels every muscle thaw, like he just stopped straining against a mesquite stump. Both cakes get tossed.

High in the bleachers, LeeRoy watches the cowgirl cheer like she's being electrocuted. Her boyfriend tears out of the chute on a wild-eyed bronc. No one counts out loud here. They do watch the clock. Until five, the rider's got a strong grip on the suitcase handle, other hand way up, his spurs tight from shoulder to rigging. Six, the bronc twists left right left then springs a back kick; the rider should get extra points for that. Seven, he's hanging on. A few beats from eight the rider flies off and lands in a roll like tumbleweed. Pickup men swoop in and set him down by the gate. He stomps away without waiting to hear his score. The girl trails behind him.

By habit LeeRoy turns to his left, wanting to tell H if that rider had leaned back more and dug in his spurs, he would have held tight and placed in the top five for sure. He wonders what H is doing. Probably tending to her garden, turning that one little rectangle into a jungle. Is she thinking about him?

Whatever he feels for H, he knows this much: she has never made him nervous. Furious, yes, shy, he's guilty, but nervous, naw, she's just H and he's the guy she glares at.

He walks around. Everyone here has someone to talk to. Even the horses have partnered up. Another stand sells bratwurst, especially good if soaked in beer before grilling. But he's got no appetite.

If bareback cain't keep him still, and bratwurst and funnel cakes cain't do a thing for him, he might as well go on back to the ranch. It's just almost noon. He'll get there well before supper. H never did sign that letter for her uncle, giving LeeRoy a reason to come back early. Then maybe he can talk her into going with him to that restaurant in Amarillo where anyone who can finish a seventy-two-ounce steak in an hour gets a free meal.

No doubt H would mouth off in her jumbled way that no one needs to devour meat the size of a baby, which would rot in his stomach for a week before completing digestion. Lee-Roy would hiss at her and chew fast and loud to block out her words. With her beside him, he just might be able to gobble down the bloody slab in its entirety.

Once Was Eleven

Hằng has spent most of her free day shooing flies from the horses, waiting for her brother to appear and be impressed with her invention of a long pole with bits of straw tied on one end. She flicks with vigor, showing the horses she understands the torment of tiny bites on innocent skin. How each mark locks in an itch that can only be relieved by setting the whole self on fire. The worms that attacked her were miniscule, though no less vicious.

She flicks and flicks, erasing images of the worms. When her brother finally emerges, eyes and cheeks puffy from oversleep, he steps straight toward his horse. Hằng coughs from across the fence. Stamps her work boots. Swings a spoon against a tin pail.

Linh the Boy has the bad manners to look annoyed before

going into the stable and returning with a bottle of oil. He rubs his horse's head, neck, shoulders. The smell crawls inside Hằng's nostrils, spicy and minty, what Bà grew at home to shoo mosquitoes. If she had known, she would have slathered the oil on the horses and saved hours of flicking. LeeRoy left without training her or so much as a whisper.

Her brother leads his horse into the stable. She refuses to call to him. All those hours together in pain under the sun should have thawed him toward her. He said nothing when she showed him drawing after drawing, but he did pocket them all. They still haven't exchanged one word.

Furious, she thinks of ripping up today's drawing. But she took time sketching *trái mận,* a crisp, watery fruit that pops into halves when pressed between palms. Linh loved the pop. Rule was he could split only the ones he would eat. But that boy, those plump little hands, and soon an entire basket of halves had to be reconstructed to appear whole. Bà would pretend to chide him, in truth nodding at his cleverness. For such a story, it took Hằng hours to calculate five sentences. She wishes Ly-Roi were here to practice sounding out the words.

Her brother is no doubt cooing to and brushing a horse already sleek as water. At times she has yearned to be his horse, then become irritated for having to resort to the thought. She would never reveal her irritation though, still treating Linh like a precious guest. Ly-Roi, instead, has absorbed more than his fair share of her temper.

She calls for Ly-Roi, knowing he's not present, but feels lighter to puff her lungs. As if in answer a vehicle turns from the main road, dragging a brown cloud along the long dirt path. "Ly-Roi!" She runs, amazed at her own elation. But inside the dispersion of dust rolls not a red truck but a low burgundy car. She retreats into the stable.

"Quick, quick, hide me."

Her brother, eyes bulging, stands between her and his beloved. Such a strange boy, first giving his name to a horse, now protecting it from the sister who has crossed the world to rescue him. She runs behind the horse.

"Never stand behind a horse," he screams, then pulls Linh the horse away. She stares in amazement: He has spoken directly to her, even if in a shout, even if his words wrap around that snorting giant. Before she could reply, Chú Quốc runs in. With him is En-Di.

"Wow, Moon, what are you wearing?" En-Di scrunches up her face toward Hằng's tied pants and stuffed boots. Along with a flouncy blue dress, En-Di flaunts boots decorated with blue birds.

Hằng turns to her uncle. *"Tell her this is what people wear to work. Really hard work."*

"You will not work when live with me. For letter, better we see a lawyer here and tell story. Can get signature stamped. Angie brought a dress. The faster we . . ."

As her uncle steps closer and louder, Hằng backs up to where En-Di is talking in involved, laughing sentences with her brother. Envy soaks into Hằng so intensely she has to pinch her arm to not shake her cousin.

"The one time I rode a horse I thought I would never walk right again," En-Di says, and rubs her cheek against the horse's neck. Hằng chides herself, why has she not thought to massage her own face there?

Her brother smiles, actually smiles, while brushing and talking. "You would have been all right if you posted. It's like sitting on a cloud for me."

Hằng realizes she should have been drawing horses, not fruit. Luring her brother with horses flying across a field, horses pawing the air, horses neck to neck, horses chewing candy, horses dirt bathing, horse horses horses. Ly-Roi should have suggested that, being the one who spat sentences at her brother hour connecting hour.

Her uncle tries to nudge Hằng and En-Di out of the stable. "Go get her dressed for the appointment," he tells his daughter.

En-Di turns to Linh. "You could board the horse near us when you come live with us."

"Why? I live here." Her brother answers evenly, an established fact.

Chú Quốc whispers so only the girls can hear, "Don't talk about that now. The judge will tell him."

En-Di shakes her head. "Shouldn't we talk to him first? And to his mother?"

Hằng is starting to really like her logical cousin.

Her uncle pushes them outside. "Go change." He's gritting his teeth.

Co-ra appears. "Ready to ride—" She chops her own sentence upon seeing them. Worry overwhelms the soft lines on her face, worry and perplexity. She probably has never witnessed so many Vietnamese under one roof.

En-Di steps up and extends a hand. So bold. "Hello, I'm Angie, his cousin. You have a great barn here."

Hằng concentrates on Co-ra's obvious panic as more of En-Di's words float to the high beams and stay. Co-ra replies, fast and punctured. It's impossible to catch more than "get out."

Co-ra stands tall and releases another typhoon, ending with "he is mine." She grabs Linh's hand and runs out, but Chú Quốc blocks them.

"We are so grateful for your care," her uncle says. "It's time to let a judge decide what's best for the boy."

Co-ra shoves her uncle, hard. Her eyes wild. Everyone is

talking at once. It's not difficult to guess what each is fighting for, even if Hằng catches only random words ejecting from any one of their throats: horse, adopted, live, died, kidnapped.

Chú Quốc shouts at Hằng, *"Tell her, tell her that her brother kidnapped our boy."*

Hằng opens her mouth. Nothing. Her voice evaporates as guilt wrings her gut. If only there weren't so much fear and anguish on Co-ra's face. Countless times Bà held that same compressed panic. When Hằng relayed a school command to report what Bà and Mother say at home. When Bà envisioned crossing the sea. When Hằng came of age with spots of blood on her undergarment.

It is the panic of a protector unable to protect.

As Co-ra stares into Hằng, her lips quiver, almost pleading, but tears refuse to drop. Her words elongate, each clear as a drop of water. "He belongs with me."

To prove it, her brother hugs Co-ra so tightly his cheekbone might snap her collarbone. In his puffy, squeezed face, safety congeals thick enough for Hằng to reach out and savor it in her palm.

She once was eleven. At eleven she had Bà and Father and Mother and brother. Her worries were reciting a poem to perfection and wondering if Bà would cook her or Linh's favorite *chè* for dessert. At eleven Linh doesn't need to know about the puppy inside Bà's calf or where Father's bones rested or how Mother floated or what Hằng witnessed crossing the world. Their uncle knows some of the stories, and he reacted as if attacked by wild dogs. At eleven she was cocooned inside spun sugar, oblivious that adults scorched their organs to prevent cracks in the many, many sweet filaments protecting her.

She smiles at Co-ra, whose eyes cling to outrage but whose cheeks surrender to curves of hope. She turns to her uncle. A deep breath, a deeper breath, then she releases a confession that should have touched air long ago.

Cute

When LeeRoy pulls up it looks for a second like a party. Everyone's outside, animated, even Mr. Morgan. But this ain't a party unless they're playing at a game where the winner screams the loudest into the most faces. H's uncle is winning, flapping both arms like a drunk traffic controller. He then drags his thrashing niece to his little car, with a girl in a short blue dress yanking on his arm.

"Whoa, easy now." LeeRoy jumps out. "If you recall, manhandling her wasn't all that successful. I thought we've done established she's a miniature adult who can stay where she pleases."

Ignoring LeeRoy, the uncle stuffs H into the backseat and turns to the crowd. "I'll be back for the boy."

Poor David is clutching onto his mama like she's the world's most powerful magnet. Cora yells, "I'm getting a restraining order against you."

Mr. Morgan pats her on the shoulder. "Now, now, let's see if we can't reason through this."

LeeRoy's words are stuttering inside him. After tormenting the three of them for the innocent act of midnight rodeoing, now all the sudden Mr. Mean is Mr. Reasonable?

H escapes and comes running over as her uncle bounds toward LeeRoy. The girl in the blue dress, as slight as H, tries to weigh the uncle down. She might as well be a bag of feathers.

The girl shines a smile on him and extends her hand. "I'm Angie. You work here?" Her grip is strong as clamps.

"Um, yeah, H and I got stuck together for the summer." LeeRoy finds himself standing straighter than usual, a blush warming his face.

"H? That's clever. I call her Moon." Angie twirls her hair. It looks soft.

Thankfully, the nuisance in his pants is distracted by all the commotion. To be safe, LeeRoy thinks of mucking and wheeling straw-stuck clumps to a manure pile. That makes two pretty girls paying him mind, in one day. Not bad for a newly minted cowboy.

H is shooting a death laser between his eyes.

"What?" He eyeballs her right back. "It's called a

conversation, where two people trade sentences without going into battle."

H shakes her head and leads her cousin away, though not before he hears Angie say, "He's cute."

Right then H turns around and stares like she's seeing through him. Her brows no longer twisted in a fit. He waves to her and expects a glare. Her cousin nudges her. To his surprise H smiles. He can't help himself, pointing to his face and shouting, "Cute!"

Too Intense

Her dad is slumped in the passenger seat, thumb and index pressing into his eyes, breaths dragging like snores.

"If your cousin had swallowed the story from long ago, the boy would be going home to us, I have no doubt about that," he says, and clamps his jaws as if controlling a howl.

When he gets this distraught, Angie knows to pop in Trịnh Công Sơn, the premier poet songwriter whose sad lyrics have always drained her dad's anger. His jawline thaws within the first few guitar picks to "Diễm Xưa."

Mưa vẫn mưa bay trên tầng tháp cổ
Dài tay em mấy thuở mắt xanh xao . . .

Angie's singing along; not every word, but for a girl who

doesn't speak Vietnamese, she's mighty impressed with her ability to croon about lost love and flying rain.

Her dad lifts his face, raises an eyebrow.

"Dad, I've been listening to this since before I could talk, and Mom told me it's always something sad about rain or pacifism or death or love and back to rain, lots of rain, like a thousand different kinds of rain."

There, she did it. He smiles.

The Vietnamese must have as many words for rain as the Eskimos have for snow. From the core word *mưa* (rain), she has looked up *mưa đá* (hail), *mưa phùn* (drizzle), *mưa rào* (shower), *mưa bong bóng* (bubble rain), *mưa li ti* (tiny rain), *mưa lớn* (heavy rain), and her dad's favorite, *mưa buồn* (sad rain).

Now her dad is talking in an even tone. "I think Hằng might be lying, saying anything to maneuver closer to the mom, thus the boy."

Angie nods. But they both know it: without Hằng's testimony, there's no need for a lawyer, much less a judge.

"We can visit them. Maybe they will visit us, once they trust you won't imprison them or something. They'll like their rooms, the dressers, the desks, the clothes, you've done a lot."

His mouth twists, not believing her yet.

"Here's the thing, Dad. Are you listening? This might be hard to hear, but you're too intense. It freaks them out. When you do it to me, it freaks me out. Chill, let them come to you. It's not like they're gonna disappear or something, right? When I dance, if I concentrate on a sequence too much, I mess up. My teacher is always telling me to let go and practice until the steps are effortless. She says no one wants to watch someone else's desperation. Maybe she's right?"

"You're still wanting to dance for a living?"

"I'm going to throw myself into it and see what happens."

For once, her dad does not launch into a lecture about frivolous dreams. He turns up the volume instead.

Chiều nay còn mưa sao em không lại
Nhớ mai trong cơn đau vùi . . .

Oh, the anguish. Her mom has said every line in every Trịnh Công Sơn song detaches muscles from bones, leaving a noodle being who can do no more than weep. No wonder during the war both sides banned the artist's songs, fearing no soldier would bother to hold a gun if he still had a breath to live for love. After the war the Communists put Trịnh Công Sơn in a labor camp, only to later anoint him a national treasure.

Angie knows plenty about the war and its aftermath. Her dad has never stopped feeling guilty that while his mother and brother suffered he was here eating too much and driving too fast. He wants to make it up to them by providing for her cousins.

"You're not thinking of talking Moon into medical school, are you? I'm pretty sure she has no interest, and forget about the boy."

A halting, divided exhale, then her dad bites his lower lip.

"Dad, did you hear me?"

He nods. "You might be right."

That was easy. Maybe he's worn out, but Angie has never gotten him to agree this fast to anything. She decides to go for it.

"Enough of this sad stuff, how about we listen to the radio for a while?"

He nods.

"How about we stop for chicken sandwiches?"

He nods again.

"How about we get me a 280Z?"

He leans toward her and intense dad returns.

Ice Pebbles

Everyone has been lovely to Hằng after her cousin took away Chú Quốc and tension. Especially Co-ra, busy scratching papers to claim her son in court. Reacting to their smiles, Hằng can barely lift her cheekbones. Only five days before Linh returns to school. Then Ly-Roi will leave as soon as his truck regains its smoothness.

What then? The question expands like the land before her.

During daylight, she can quiet the unknown by forcing the practical. Regular workers soon will return for the couch, the horses, the life. So she's arranging sentences to talk her way into being useful, perhaps ask to cultivate a garden, to sell vegetables, anything. Perhaps she could nail together a shelter on one end of the porch. If not, in a corner in the stable. There's always the vast land itself. Perhaps a hut made from scattered planks and leveled under one of those thorn-infested trees. Or near that stubborn stump whose roots remain entangled within the earth. As long as she sees her brother every day, it matters not how she works or where she finds rest.

But there's the quiet dark. Those stretches before sleep when blood gushes through her veins and she has to open her mouth to breathe. Nervous about whether she will be permitted to stay near her brother, she feels vulnerable. That's when memories surge, wading through mental torrents to reinstate their claim.

The younger monk hid just below the sea, breathed through a hollow reed. Liquid salt wiggled into nose, into throat. An acid cruelty belittling thirst. Waves thrashed legs against coral. Ribbons of blood diluted to pink. More ribbons, more red. Strips turned rose then paler and paler before blending into the blue green.

In these gray hours she yearns for the assurance of work: horses, chickens, the garden. Anything, so memories have no space to circulate.

Today they will harvest the precious melons, so fragrant a floral cling floats into the house. Tomorrow they will sell the fruit at a market called a fair, which Ly-Roi explained is a celebration for the end of summer. It sounds demanding: music, people, laughter, the sun, the smells. Even so, she'll go because her brother will be near.

The air is crisp, landing on her skin not as insect bites of heat but as cool kisses before rain. Ly-Roi and her brother, burping a gut-puffy breakfast, join her on the porch. Ông Mó-gần has added to the table flat round cakes soaked with syrup, tasting of sweetened clouds. Even so, by habit, she stopped eating as soon as she felt full, allowing her mind to catch up to her stretched stomach.

Hằng begins today's story. Linh listens narrow-browed as she pronounces five excruciatingly molded sentences. As always, Ly-Roi rescues them, restating her tale of Linh's favorite snack after napping. Everybody napped back home, even Bà. When they woke, the sugar cane peddler would know to appear, calling out in the clammy heat that pieces already stripped and cubed and bagged awaited on ice. Linh chewed each cube until his tiny taste buds absorbed every hint of cold liquid sugar. Only then would he spit out pulp seemingly gnashed by steel teeth.

Linh stares. Hằng wants to shake him, to pry words from his mouth, to make him remember anything at all. But Ông Mó-gần appears and is hiding something behind his back. The sky opening on his face.

"Ta da."

He presents a rough-skinned melon large as a head. With a knife like her own, still at her ankle, he halves the cantaloupe on his palm. The gut seeds are saved in a bucket. Peach-hue juice drips between his fingers as he has Linh hold one half. The other is sliced into four crescent moons.

Crisp and sweet, scented with sunlight. Yelps of joy from all of them. But then Ông Mó-gân points to wooden crates stacked high. Time to work. "Be careful. Ten to a crate. Do not bruise any. We sell each for three dollars."

Ly-Roi shakes his head. "I've never heard of a three-dollar melon."

"Mine are special." Ông Mó-gân speaks no other explanation.

Each cantaloupe weighs as if lead is hidden inside. An arm-length vine is left on each fruit to prolong the mother supply of sugar. Ông Mó-gân has many other tricks for growing prized melons, but he keeps them as deep inside as Hǎng guards her memories.

When they have filled half the crates, drops fall from the sky. It's so disorienting to feel rain here she is instantly transported back to Sài Gòn. Except there, rain would be hot, soft, melting into the dust cloud at her feet. Another drop, then another. The air cools, fast. The drops turn solid and bounce off the scruffy skin of cantaloupes.

Ông Mó-gân shouts something, causing Ly-Roi and her brother to pull the filled crates into the stable and drag out plastic drums saved for collecting rain. Hằng flips the lids, which catch their share too.

The drops now land with force on her head. Each one a pebble thrown from the sky.

Co-ra appears, animated about something that sounds like "hell," but Hằng suspects she's not talking about devils and fire.

Ly-Roi laughs, gathering ice lumps in his palm. "You ever seen these?" He pops one into his mouth. "Waste not, want not."

The pebbles fall faster, harder. No one is laughing now. Certainly not Ông Mó-gần, frantic to throw every last rock into his rain barrels. The next wind brings drops the size of kumquats. They hurt.

"Dadgum it," Ly-Roi yells. "Get us some helmets."

Ông Mó-gần has no concern for his or anyone else's hatless heads. He drags plastic sheets wide as two blankets from somewhere and motions that the covers should be thrown over the vines. They try.

Now icy quail eggs bombard them. Hằng imagines blue-purple bumps rising on her scalp. Her brother has quit and is in the stable soothing his dry yet stomping horse, who is frightened of the *plocks* on the roof. Hằng stops to listen. The horse is right. It does sound menacing, an attack from the clouds.

Ông Mó-gần and Ly-Roi struggle to throw a plastic blanket

over a too-tall stalk. Hằng runs to get a ladder. Coming back, one hand dragging the ladder, other hand protecting her eyes, she slips and falls on her back. Baby breaths, palms sheltering her face while she lies motionless on a hump in the earth. From above, nature hurls rocks with hundreds of arms. By the time Ly-Roi runs over, her back is on fire.

Hằng jumps up and screams. She never screams. Not on the boat, not on the island.

"Stay still, H, you've got fire ants." Ly-Roi grips the panels of her shirt and rips off all the buttons, then he peels off the wet sleeves as if they were skin. He thrashes the shirt before turning it into a washcloth, wiping her back in harsh panic. "You hurt?"

Hundreds of miniscule flames explode into an itchy inferno. Rosy bites inflate on her naked arms. Hằng imagines the same dots are rising on her back, which is covered only by a thin layer of undershirt. These bumps anchor above dozens of red tracks zigzagging beneath her skin. That's what Ly-Roi sees. So does Ông Mó-gần, so does Co-ra. Hundreds more lines run under her clothing from her throat to her toes. A vile, subterranean map to nowhere.

Hằng snatches back the long-sleeved shirt and struggles to put it on. Impossible against wet cotton and shame. She runs. Co-ra calls out, "Honey, you don't have to . . ."

Hằng's work boots crunch ice balls; her ankles twist like

caught fish. She runs. The shirt over her head, its prized sleeves flapping and teasing.

Stomps close in behind her. Without turning around she yells, "Nô phó-lô."

He follows her, still.

Upper Arm Against Hers

LeeRoy knows better than to yell for her to stop, betting she'll turn right around and ram him. Can't be careful enough, having seen that temper of hers once too many. Jeez Louise, that girl can run, slip-sliding on hail, no less. At least he had the sense to hold on to the tarp. Spread above his head, it makes for a not-too-shabby flying raincoat. He's not sure what he saw beneath the ant bites, but one thing's for sure, H did not want anybody eyeing her business. And another thing, he was a fool to have thought those lines were tattoos.

H is soaked but somehow has struggled her sleeves back on. She runs, clasping together the front panels of her shirt in place of buttons.

They keep running. Ice pings off the tarp covering him but pounds her exposed self. She slips. LeeRoy catches up and holds the plastic sheet over her. Surely she appreciates having a personal umbrella. To be safe he says nothing, which is excruciating, given the hundreds of questions any right-minded human would be conjuring up.

H gets up and keeps right on running. They're in open country so Lord knows how long this foolishness will go on. It's downright cold now. He about twists an ankle. These complaints he keeps to himself. No point in adding to the drama H is inflating all by herself.

They keep running. His thighs pulsate inside water-heavy jeans. His heart drums enough to wake the dead. And of course his stomach is growling, having burned through every bit of breakfast. LeeRoy runs and dreams of hot cocoa. Of waffles and strawberries, his father's specialty. Of smoked ribs, his mother's. Of an entire key lime pie, topped with LeeRoy's egg whites whipped until they are as sturdy as a helmet. If he were to go on home after Red got fixed up, he would never have to pine for food again.

But he's in no rush to head back to Austin, back to Plan B because Yale didn't even get a start. His parents have counted on UT as backup since kindergarten. If not Austin, then where? Then what? Sometimes he wishes he were as focused as H. She's going to stay near her brother, and no uncle, guilt, unknown, fear, or whatnot can alter her primal vow.

"Hey, slow down, this ain't no way to treat a buddy who has

seen you through all kinds of hell this summer," LeeRoy yells. She keeps going. Fast for a little bird. It's really boring, this constant running. Even the hail has gotten bored, switching to plump, heavy drops. He tries to cheer himself up, thinking it could be so much worse. They could be running in a heat wave and about to drop dead; they could be in the path of a wild boar stampede; they could have fallen into a cactus pit and come out like porcupines. Try as he might, he's not at all uplifted. They're bad off.

Suddenly the figure of H stops. He catches up and has never been so grateful to eyeball a gigantic hole in the ground. A stunning one at that, all them rocky layers of yellow, pink, purple, red, and brown against bushes, cedars, and no doubt pesky mesquites. In the gray sky a tall rock juts out, shaped just like a lighthouse.

H bends over, panting, palms on her knees, mouth open, her heart about to jump out of her throat. That's about where he's at too. LeeRoy reasons it's all right to start in on her, seeing as she doesn't have anything left for yelling or slamming.

"You about done for, H?"

She keeps mouth breathing and clutching the panels of her shirt. He can see her heart pounding beneath two layers of cotton. The tarp he widens to cover her too. The rain has turned into a cold, fast drip.

"Figure we should be heading on back?" He tries to sound

casual, as if either way is fine. "What do you say we walk it instead of hauling like a coyote is at our heels?"

In answer, she squats to the muddy ground. Good God Almighty, what choice does he have but to spread the tarp partly on the ground for them to sit on and the rest pulled over their heads. It does feel really good to sit, even if on top of icy lumps.

"Don't worry, in no time our heat will melt the ice right down." He squishes around for good measure, thinking she would join him. It's not every day they get to melt ice with their bee-hinds. But nothing. She stares into the expanse like she's seeing something altogether different from horizontal stripes deepening to the horizon. The cold doesn't seem to bother her even though goosebumps inflate on the back of her hands. She keeps her shirt so tightly bound hardly any other skin shows.

He tries again. "Not to be a party pooper, but we need to get you dry and warm. Then how about some hot cocoa? I bet Mr. Morgan has a can stashed away somewhere. I'm cold. Aren't you cold?"

In answer, she bends her legs to her chest and rests her chin on her knees. Chest covered, she releases her shirt to wrap her arms around herself. Deep breaths. All the while staring into the gray-lit canyon. As if he isn't there.

LeeRoy leans over and nudges her ever so slightly, his upper arm against hers. To his surprise, heat transfers between them. She doesn't nudge back, but she doesn't move away either. If anything, she hugs her legs tighter and takes longer breaths. He too wraps his arms around his knees, keeping their touch.

"C'mon, H, we can come back when it's a nice day and get our fill of a sunset or something. Keep sitting here and you're liable to catch pneumonia. Lord knows what your uncle would do to me then. Ready?"

He tries to stand and pull the tarp with him but she lumps down and says, "Thóc mo. Ai lai-kờ ít."

"You'd like me to talk more? That's a first."

"Bờ-li-sì thóc."

Lured by her "please," LeeRoy finds himself sitting back down. No more lumps, just squishy mud warmed by his truly. He stares into the canyon, upper arm against hers, and knows he's got plenty to say.

"Just so happens I did my senior thesis on the geological, historical, and political significance of the Palo Duro Canyon. I've got enough for a book. First off, what you're looking at used to be an ocean all them millions of years ago."

"Ố-sần?" She tilts her face to meet his. He feels a shiver run through her arm.

"Yes ma'am, ocean. See, geologists have determined that right here was a sea, rivers, floodplains, lakes, and swamps. The paleontologists came in and found all sorts of vertebrate fossils. After testing the strata exposed in the walls, it's understood that the oldest rocks on the canyon floor go back two hundred and forty million years and every layer tells its own history. The youngest rocks of course are at the canyon rim and we're sitting on quartz, sandstone, and limestone. On down you have what's called massive micaceous, quartz sandstone, and conglomerate, also interbedded shale and mudstone, next is variegated shale and mudstone in addition to quartz and calcite that they call sugar sand. The floor has interbedded siltstone, shale, and claystone, then finally gypsum."

LeeRoy figures he'll bore her into standing up and running away from the thousands of facts lodged in his brain. But her upper arm relaxes against his. Her chin sinks a little more into her knees. Back to staring, she keeps taking them deep gulps of air. Sometimes she closes her eyes then forces them open again.

"Thóc mo."

"You serious, H? Talk more?"

"Kíp thóc-kinh."

Something breaks in her voice, soft, barely hanging on. He can't see her whole face but a side view is plenty. One eye, heavy lid, and so sad it's got to be covering up something. Sensing she needs his nonsense talking more than he needs to get warm, LeeRoy hunkers down on the squishy ground.

"If you want me to keep talking, I'll talk. Do you know that the Indians made good use of this canyon for twelve thousand years? Hikers today still find burned boiling pebbles and hearth stones and flint flakes and all kinds of artifacts, especially near the wet portions of the main canyon and tributaries . . ."

Smooth Lullaby of Buzzes

Ocean. The word sparkles amid Ly-Roi's torrent of hisses unfurling and curling about her like waves. Hằng can't understand a third of his words. Nonetheless, they soothe. His voice is lower, tone even, sentences clean. Unspoken are the numerous extra phrases that he claims make him a cowboy but only entangle in her mind. He sounds like a schoolbook, something to learn, something to contemplate.

As she listens, a crimson line flashes across a pale, thin neck. Yet her throat is not constricting, her intestines not looping toward nausea. She is able to endure a surge of memory and still swallow wide gulps of air. Releasing slowly.

When Ly-Roi pauses, she nudges him to keep talking. She wants to soak in every *s* and *ed* and the forever confusing "a," "an," and "the." She craves his smooth lullaby of buzzes, needs his bees to hover over images that are reasserting fast and stubborn. It matters not that she's wet and cold, having already survived an ocean where every drop was wet and cold.

A body drifted down and away from her, drifted until it touched bottom. Somewhere between Việt Nam and Thái Lan. The body rolling on sand and wavy plants and attracting the nibbles of fish.

Such images keep pricking at her, daring her to stare into them. The exhaustion of suppressing stabs of memory while managing her impulse to forget, to divert, to plot, to reclaim.

It's time to remember, in this most unlikely land, inside this most unlikely rain, next to this most unlikely boy. She feels safe, the safest since leaving Bà. Ly-Roi can't help but be kind from the core of his gut. *Tốt từ trong bụng ra.* Bà would be proud she chose wisely.

Five bloody lines down a sun-scorched back. In return, the pirate slashed the older monk's robe and blouses. His machete then edged beneath the bound cloth, his face gorged with surprise. The older monk sidestepped, darting fingers toward the pirate's eyes. The younger monk jumped on the pirate's bleeding back. Bit, shook, spat flesh. Blood on the tongue, blood encircling lips. The pirate howled. A red line plumped on a pale, thin neck. A wilted body, flung by its crimson neck into the sea. The younger monk, crimson mouthed, jumped in after the body of the older monk.

Hằng holds her breath. Pinches her thumb. It hurts. Good, she can still feel. Exhales. She has remembered and has not melted. Ly-Roi's upper arm still warm against hers, his voice steadily releasing buzzing bees and alarmed snakes and baritone bullfrogs. If he keeps talking, she can make herself chisel into these memories and perhaps dislodge their anchor from the back of her skull. Bà always said meditation on the most unpleasant images—a rotting corpse, the fury of a stranger—will dissolve disgust into vapor. Eventually.

Another deep breath. It's time. It's time to stop distancing. Call the characters by their true names. Ease her heart into withstanding the entirety of what happened on the boat, what happened on the island.

I kicked and reached but Mother floated away, eyes closed, shaved head bobbing. The bound cloth still protecting her breasts. If not for the red line across her throat, she could have been asleep. Sinking, I discarded my robe, which billowed like a cloud toward Mother. I bounced upward. No matter how I reached, no matter how I kicked, Mother grew smaller as bitter salt seared into my eyes. A smeared final glimpse of Mother as my robe escorted her down.

Air. Lungs burned as I swallowed waves. I grabbed onto silky currents. How I yearned for something solid to cling to. The needling cold didn't degrade me as much as the water's formless weight. My arms and legs flapped like a crazed wind-up toy, only to grab onto more freezing boundlessness. So I forced into my mind floats the size of hills, a cement patio anchored to the ocean floor, trees with roots swiveled into the core of the earth. I paddled. I breathed.

Ly-Roi has stood up, hovering over her with the tarp turned into wings. He pulls one of her arms.

She clutches his hand, remains seated. She pierces into him, unblinking, "Du thóc, Ai bét-tờ."

Lighter Gray

Doggone it, what choice does he have but to plop back down. She shouldn't be facing him with those lips, half pleading, half determined, and spouting off that his talking makes her feel better. Only a devil-hearted cowboy could resist. Besides, he likes her grip, such heat against his cold skin. He hopes she's not working up a fever that likely will send her uncle into a conniption. That man finds out about every little thing.

"I'll keep talking if that's what you want, but you even listening?"

She nods, turning back to staring into far stretches of the canyon. It has stopped raining, so at least his arms can rest from umbrella duty. With the entire tarp on the ground, he lies down. It feels really good. Muddy, soft, and cool. He stares at a lighter gray sky.

"As I was saying, Colonel Mackenzie followed the guides and led his troops down to the canyon bottom, betting that all sorts of Comanches were down there. It was a surprise, all right, and the village was full of women and children and horses. The Comanche warriors had to flee, trying to save everybody and thousands of horses. So Mackenzie destroyed the camp and supplies that would have seen them through the winter. Lots of gunfire. Mackenzie got his men back up to the rim and all in all, 1,448 horses were captured.

"I will always remember that number, 1,448 horses, all grazing in one place. Can you imagine? The prized horses were given to the Tonkawa guides. There weren't that many human casualties in the Battle of Palo Duro, but Mackenzie ordered 1,048 horses shot after driving them to the Tule Canyon. All them bloated carcasses. Awful stuff. After that, it was pretty much the end of the Indians in the Panhandle. The buffaloes were already done in, then their horses and supplies. There wasn't a lot left to do but go into the reservations. Awful, awful extermination."

H looks over at him, her brows pinched. "Sót hó-sì?"

"I'm afraid so, all 1,048 horses shot and done for."

She sighs, goes back to whatever is so fascinating in the distance. He waits for it, and sure enough she says, "Thóc mo."

What the hell? He does as requested and talks some more.

The Island

My lungs found air. An empty but capped plastic oil jug bobbed within reach. Clutched it, bounced, waves served as feet. In the distance, silhouettes jumped into the sea as our fishing boat burned. Much laughter from the pirates, whose boat sped away amidst screeches of the engine and screams of captured girls. One long-haired silhouette leaped overboard. I counted eight dark heads atop the sea.

My feet grazed sand. Solid, grainy, ticklish. Such joy to stagger, then crawl, then shed my entire body of the sea. Full weight pressing on palms, on knees. I rolled onto land and threw up.

Other tattered bodies crawled on land. Brown beings ran toward us. Without strength to scream, I curled into a pill bug, arms helmeting my head.

"Không sao, không ai làm gì cháu đâu." A female voice,

southern accent, flew out of a seemingly benevolent gut, repeat-
ing, "Don't worry, no one will harm you."

Remaining curled, I peeked. A woman, smeared in flaking
mud from crown to toes, even on her eyelids, lifted me by my arm.
I would know she was Vietnamese even if she had not spoken.
High forehead, almond eyes, sharp cheekbones, full lips. Her iron
arms, calloused hands surprised me. She was used to work, used
to strife.

So unlike Mother, who quoted poetry and attended to her
beauty and seemed to lean against Father for strength. And yet
she scraped the pirate with her nails. Her throat was slashed
because of me.

The woman and an equally muddy helper dragged me to
shade. As if by magic, a young coconut punctured with two holes
popped into the air. Juice, sweet with a linger of tree fat. I had for-
gotten such a treasure existed. Sugar overpowered salt until every
taste bud bloomed. My eyes closed.

I awakened to hands slathering cool mud over my entirety.
It was dusk, when mosquitoes fat as flies begin their hunts. They
shrieked in frustration, demanding a feast, but the hands worked
fast providing armor as I drank more sweetness.

The other eight survivors, equally masked, began calling for
their own. One man patted every muddy face, frantic for his wife
and two young sons. He plunged back into the sea, diving to look

for them amid swirls of diluted earthy brown. No one had the quickness or the strength to stop him. A mother wailed for her children. A young boy scanned the sea for his father. A long-haired girl close to my age whimpered for her grandmother. The captain of our fishing boat lamented, "I ask for everyone's forgiveness." He disappeared inside a thicket of green.

Muddy, damp faces spoke the names of those floating at the ocean's depth, or even worse, those inside the pirates' clutches. There had been fifty-seven on a boat meant for ten. The vigil took time. I added Mother's name, Đỗ thị Mỹ Thu. As soon as I spoke, whispers confirmed that I was a girl. Maybe those on the boat always knew but allowed Mother and me the false safety of our disguise.

A savory smoke rose and my stomach convulsed from hunger. On a wild banana leaf, an offering of a grilled fish the size of my palm. I was made to chew slowly, a thumbnail morsel at a time, waiting to understand if my stomach will accept flaky fish, crunchy scales, chewy eyeballs, and a tail that shattered like a firework. I felt lucky to receive another coconut, lucky to lie down on palm fronds.

My stomach rejected every bite of fish, every drop of sweet water, also emptied of every remnant of the ocean. Undaunted, more muddy hands offered more grilled fish, more coconut. This time I entered sleep with a calm belly.

Hằng's stomach drums as she licks her lips, prompting Ly-Roi to jump up and pull at her, listing food after food that they should be eating right now.

"Du gô." She tells him to go, not meaning it. The warmth inside his grip, the rhythm of his breaths, have become as necessary as her own skin.

She yanks him back to sitting. He grumbles and sighs. It matters not what he's saying. As long as he stays and talks.

Next morning I awakened to screams of hải tặc, hải tặc, pirates, pirates. Fingers pointed, voices alarmed as we ran toward the hills and wondered why pirates would harm us on land. Women and girls were shoved inside rock crevices. Mine also held the girl who jumped from the pirates' boat. Her grandmother had watched over Mother and me. The rock walls, slimy and damp, stank of rotting crabs. A light opposite the sliver entrance roared with waves, the way back to the sea.

Someone tossed into our cave two long reeds, hollow, alongside instructions to jump if found. Stay under and breathe and drift until rescued through sticks poking above water. Do not let the pirates see you. Do not let the pirates see you. The last warning was repeated until it encircled us like pythons.

Lying down, Hằng tries to slow memories sitting like a house on her chest. She keeps her shirt buttoned by hand. She takes tiny breaths, forcing into her mind something happy.

What would she yearn for if life had granted her a warm, indulgent past? What if the last six years were simply a continuation of family, school, friends, drawing, and studying? What would be left to want?

Blank. She tries imagining something simple, a bowl of *cháo*, thickened with bone broth and scallions. Then sleep.

As soon as her eyes close, his buzzing lullaby stops. She jolts back to sitting as Ly-Roi stirs and twitches. Pulling his arm once more, her eyes widen and entreat him to keep talking.

She knows to add a smile.

Sappiness

For once, LeeRoy figures he might be all talked out. Told her so. But H is stubborn. Plopped there like it's the most logical thing in the world to hand your body over to nature and hope for the best. He half wishes it would start hailing again, great big bombers, forcing her to shelter like an owl at high noon.

"I bet Mr. Morgan is cooking up some kind of scrumptious lunch, maybe chili with corn chips." He stands. "Fine, chips are too much to hanker for, but our cranky boss does fire up a mean chili."

Instead of standing, H points to something and smiles even bigger. Darn it if she doesn't have a right dimple. Why had he not noticed until now? Of course, she's never smiled this long and deeply before. LeeRoy follows her index finger, and sure enough there's a mouse twitching out of a hole in a hill.

Man, just his luck that H has got bionic eyes, the mouse blending right into white-gray-brown rocks.

"That there is a Palo Duro mouse, I swear it doesn't exist anywhere else on God's green earth. They only get to be four inches, with a tail just as long, and they love to squeeze into crevices in the canyon walls. Good luck to their predators. And you'll love this, they eat mostly seeds. This one is probably sniffing out all the seed droppings the hail brought down and deciding whether it's hungry enough to risk being a snack for a rattlesnake."

H keeps up her grin. Who knew she has a soft spot for mice? They're cute and all, with a twitchy reddish-brown face and pudgy white belly, but nothing worth sitting on mud and shivering for.

Now H points at a horned lizard. He tells her it's a threatened species. She points at a ladybug, green and yellow, at a beetle, black with horns.

"C'mon, H, you know how many little things are living it up in this here canyon?"

She doesn't answer, keeps pointing. He spills out the facts. That's what he gets for having a memory like Krazy Glue. Once he reads something, it sticks. It would serve her right if a bobcat comes out. That'll get her up and running right quick.

But truth is, he does like seeing her happy. Somehow, that

is taking precedence over what would make him happy, namely a gorged belly and long, warm days roaming rodeos. What has happened to him? How did he turn into such a sap? And his sappiness might be hitting overdrive: starting to feel lucky he got to hang with her for the summer.

As LeeRoy sits and talks on about roadrunners, he's not altogether sure she's listening. So still, chin to bent knees, staring into the damp canyon, once again mulling over something he altogether can't see. But God forbid if he should hush up.

The Cave

Inside our tiny, slimy, dark cave, we both scratched. Hundreds of crawling somethings burned like arrows as they burrowed beneath skin. Our fingernails sawed against mud and skin and blood and muscles. I growled, quietly.

Outside the cave, the world was set on fire. Smoke and suffocation, as if red pepper sauce were flicked into eyes, matches were lit inside nostrils. I clutched the girl's hand, each of us ready with our reed, stepping toward thuds of waves. She yanked free, mumbling "Never again the sea," then ran through smoke into flames. Pirates shouted, the girl screamed. I jumped into foam.

Waves slammed me against rocks, shocked away the itches, dissolving my muddy armor. Salt wiggled into nose, into throat. An acid cruelty building into an instant thirst. Coral sliced into legs. Eyes squeezed against pain, I imagined ribbons of blood diluted to pink, more ribbons, more red, as strips turned rose then paler and paler before blending into the blue green.

My head exposed itself. Such pleasure to breathe through my nose. I heard screams among thrashing waves. Not possible, but anguish flooded the world nonetheless. Plunged back under. Made myself stay inside water. Endless passage of time as my lips shriveled while fingers clamped onto the reed, my one chance for air, for safety. Was it possible to sleep while engulfed within a sea? Seemingly a day a night another day, only to be told later the devils left within an hour. I surrendered to the currents, at times opening my eyes to see what creature stabbed dozens of holes every time my body bashed against rocks. Hard purple balls the size of fists, covered in nails. Pointy ends waiting.

My reed was yanked. I was dragged and eventually touched sand, was led toward a women's corner blanketed in broad leaves and warmed by circles of ground fire. The long-haired girl lay on her stomach, banana leaves as a bed, a palm frond covering her bottom. Her back was charred and sandy, a gathering of blood trickled to her knees, beginning between her legs. She gnawed her clenched fist.

Muddy women washed her back with coconut water, our only liquid without salt, trickling away each grain of sand to expose pink flesh beneath blackened skin. They applied a gooey ointment of forest medicine. When they started to lift the palm frond, the girl squirmed and sucked one shushing breath. They let her be. Wait, they told each other, until she has reclaimed her presence. One woman fanned away mosquitos, another dripped coconut water upon her lips. All the while the girl whimpered.

Each Inhale, Each Exhale

LeeRoy has never seen H so downtrodden. With anyone else, it would be downright proper to hug it out and offer, "It'll be all right." With her, though, he's not dumb enough to test a hug. And whatever she is seeing with those faraway eyes won't turn out all right just because he says so.

With the rain gone, the sun is fighting through the clouds. Soon humidity will grab ahold of him and eat up what little energy he has left. They have to get on back. And it's a given mosquitoes will sense blood and, finding perfect puddles for breeding, suck them dry.

"Uh, H? How about . . ."

He stops himself. She's hugging her knees as if squeezing blood from them. She sighs, just once, but heavy enough to squash a barn. LeeRoy hasn't got the slightest idea what will help, so he keeps at the one thing she's asked for.

"Bet you don't know that longhorns live here too. An official state-recognized herd! The Spaniards brought cattle to Texas in the 1500s and plenty escaped and took their chances in the great outdoors, like we're doing now except better equipped to get pelted with hail and all. I mean, they can sleep standing up so who cares if the ground is wet. Did you know that cattle lying down means it's gonna rain soon? Anyhoo, their descendants roamed all over Texas until the early settlers rounded them up and made a good living. A bull can fetch a thousand now, can you believe it? They are hardy, I'll give them that, surviving on nothing but poor pastureland. I'm betting they have the toughest neck muscles in the world, lugging around them horns."

LeeRoy gets on all fours and swings his head like an overburdened longhorn, mooing for effect.

Nothing. Man, she's a tough audience.

LeeRoy peers into her far-off face, where even her blinks seem immobilized. It might be best just to sit and breathe with her, matching each inhale, each exhale. Like her, he sits with legs bent, chin on his knees, arms in a wrap-around. Their upper arms touch once again. He leans into her. She leans back, so slightly. Not much, but enough to keep him there.

The Worms

As shock flattened, itches resurged. How I scratched. An herbalist gave me and the girl a strangling drink bitter of every herb, leaf, bark. Drowsy, my will receded to the sky. I let them unravel salty undergarments, then lay me down on my own layers of leaves.

The girl and I squirmed with itches, scraping arms, nape, sides. Soon, twine tied our fingers. Two women fanned away mosquitoes while others stone-sharpened hairpin tips, dipped in coconut water boiled in their own shells on fires fueled by their own husks. Tiny airholes were pricked on our skin touching the leafy beds. It felt ticklish, compared to the holes made from the thorns on purple creatures. Once we were deemed to have enough openings, hot water expanded under us, wilting green banana leaves.

The herbalist whispered that they crave warmth, abandoning hot for hotter, slimy walls for our blood, our blood for boiled water. *What are they? No answer, just more liquid, more steam. Beneath my skin, slitherings began slow and continuous and so itchy my eyes burned. Finally, something bored through my back to plunge into the bath. I was turned on my stomach, where coral had gashed thighs and shins, where purple creatures seared many holes. No need for pin pricks. More slitherings, more crazed itching. Until a soft dullness of nothing. I was instructed to stand, to witness hundreds of tiny white worms swimming in elation. The water was released while writhing bodies remained captured. The leafy mattress was coiled and thrown into flames.*

The girl would not turn over, would not get up. Water was poured on her seared back, pink flesh exposed. No need for pinpricks. Liquid and heat over and over until tiny white heads sniffed the air and crawled onto her steaming skin, following the red tracks they had inked. Each worm was picked off and sizzled in the fire. The girl did not sigh, did not stir. She did stop whimpering.

Someday

H has got her forehead on her knees. LeeRoy hears quick, stuttering breaths, stifling a full-on cry. She seems as bad off as a fox gnawing a trapped leg. If she would look up, he could point to the sun peeking through and black birds giddy at the bonanza of exposed worms.

"C'mon, H, things surely were rough but you don't gotta stay tough. You gotta right to cry, and Lord knows I've tried . . ."

LeeRoy claps and lets out a tight-gut laugh. Without even trying, he's rapped.

I know enough
to know it was rough
so you don't gotta stay tough.
Poof oof ugh ugh ugh.

Go on and cry,
only right that you try
to let red soak into your eyes
and release everything to the sky.
Poof oof ugh ugh ugh.

He stops. No one needs to clue him in on how bad that was. But it does get H to peer right at him. Her eyes are red and puffy, but by God she's half smiling.

"Du rai pô-ểm?"

"If you want to call that a poem, then sure thing, I wrote a poem."

"Bét pô-ểm." Her eyes, still red, are laughing.

"Bad? If you think you can do better, go at it, missy."

H gets quiet again. Oh no, she can't go back to that eerie, distant stare. There's only so much he can take. But H stands, one hand still gathering the neck of her shirt. LeeRoy jumps up. Yes, this is more like it. She's looking at the ground. Fine, maybe for a direction to head on back. Then she picks up a stick with the free hand. Not really strong enough to be a walking stick, but she's tiny, maybe that's all she needs.

She starts writing on the soggy ground, line after line. Lee-Roy makes out "homes, bones, gold, karma, skin, kind." The tiny marks over vowels in "*hải tặc*" sink under the weight of mud. She scribbles out that phrase. Soon all her words rejoin the muddy slake and she throws the stick in a huff.

LeeRoy stumbles on a way home. "Know what would work a whole lot better? Pencil and paper. And you know where I have plenty of both? That's right, back with reliable Red. Let's go check on her, no telling what the hail has inflicted on my poor truck."

Thinking of Red getting pelted and abused gets LeeRoy so agitated he starts walking away from the canyon. Everything has a time limit. H's just ran out. It's Red's turn.

He looks back at H. "Well, c'mon, it's not like your clothes are going to dry themselves."

H's saying something.

"Speak up, will ya?"

She doesn't. Her lips keep moving. LeeRoy throws up his hands. "After all this time, now you decide to tell me something?" What choice does he have but to walk on back.

Even next to her, he has to lean down to hear. H talks/sings clear and sure, accounting for every contraction and past tense and plural in a steady rhythm. Every syllable gets released like molasses, turning her into some other speaker altogether. Instead of pissed-off snakes, her *s* sounds enter the world as slowly leaking tires.

They ranked us low, they con-fis-ca-ted our homes,
still we claimed Father's bones and fled toward
*   unknowns.*
They ripped away our gold, they slashed our fa-mi-lies,
still we bit and jumped and knew karma will avenge
*   upon fi-na-li-ties.*
They bored into our flesh, they scorched red roads on our
*   skin,*
still I find Brother and our future will begin.
For every stomach that reeks along-side cruel minds,
there's one like yours that can't help but be kind.

LeeRoy jumps up and down, slapping his thighs. "H, you've done rapped. Slow as all get-go, but it's a genuine rap. You're surely the first Vietnamese rapper in all of Texas."

H stands before him, blinking. LeeRoy forces himself to stay still and not scare her. Her rap replays in his mind. Like with reading, once he hears something it sticks. Every half line hints at hours of backstory. He could soak through two, three hailstorms with her and still not get at all that's scrambled inside.

LeeRoy joins her blinks. They share slight smiles. When H takes a deep breath, so does he. When she releases one of her long sighs, he does too. He instinctively knows to keep quiet.

He's getting it now. Gets that he can't push her to reveal herself any more than he can push away his gut need to be a cowboy. It will take time.

Some things you don't poke at. Someday she might want to flesh out that rap poem to someone. And if he's around, attentive, that someone might be him. Never will he ask about them red lines on her skin. Someday she might need to tell that long story. And maybe . . .

She's something to behold, this girl who's staring into his eyeballs even though he's got a good foot on her. Her hair a mess, her complexion pale green and goose-pimpled, her clothes soaked and shabby. But Lord, she dazzles.

It's still not the right time for a hug. He bends down and fake punches her in one shoulder. She tilts her head to tame all manner of thought that must be clanging around in there. Then she balls up a fist and hooks it toward him. The punch lands on his bicep with just the right amount of weighty softness.

The sound of a truck. LeeRoy turns to see Cora and David waving and now honking.

LeeRoy bends and points to his back. To his surprise, H hops on. Even more of a surprise, she giggles as he slips and slides. Giggles something fierce, like she's once again a little girl.

PART III

the butterfly

Inside a Face

Hair damp, Hằng shivers as she sits in Co-ra's kitchen. But she will not show displeasure. After all, following the hailstorm yesterday, Co-ra pampered her with a bath and pajamas. Then, to Hằng's delight, Co-ra invited her into a room next to Linh and announced, "Let's give your nose a break from Mr. Morgan's couch."

Twice, Hằng drifted from her bed and watched sleep envelop her brother, whose door stayed open. In the moonlight she saw faint traces of the boy who once adored her; his lips parted, a snore whistled, eyelashes light as hope napped on his cheekbones. She willed forth magical words that would lure Linh to their uncle's. Nothing came to her. Bà would have known what to say.

"Sugar, you're about to not recognize yourself," Co-ra says

from behind, clicking scissors. "What I wouldn't give for more than your five choppy inches. Though you make it up in texture, that's for sure, so soft and sleek and thick. I could bite you I'm so envious."

Another talker. Hằng is grateful. Without releasing one word, she has a conversation. This one has her heartbeats accelerating, her eyes blinking.

"No need to be nervous, I've got gentle hands."

Hằng wonders how long Co-ra's generosity will last, wonders if she's completing the final act by polishing Hằng into a shiny girl for the fair. Then what? The short question irritates her like gnats. Then what?

Co-ra comes around, leans down so they're almost nose to nose. "A pixie cut is our best bet, sweetie."

Their foreheads bump when Linh comes in and yells, "MaaaaMaaaa, why can't I help load the cantaloupes? I crated them and got pelted with hail like everyone else, why can't I, pleeeeease?"

"You hush up." She shakes the scissors at him. "Your job right now is to get dressed and stay looking nice. Don't go getting sweaty on me, it's going to get over ninety today. You and this one here will become easy on the eyes even if I have to sit on the both of ya."

"MaaaaaMaaaaa!"

"There's ten dollars in it for you if you do what I ask and don't annoy me for the rest of the morning. Now, git."

Linh slumps away without once looking at his sister. He has to thaw at some point, Hằng tells herself. She's the only one who looks like him around here. That has to matter.

Co-ra keeps talking as she yanks, cuts, and twists. A smelly paste is smeared over the entirety of Hằng's head. Next, an attack on eyelashes, eyelids, eye rims, lips, lip rims, cheekbones, chin, and even throat.

"You have great bones, my girl. Wait till you see what else I'm capable of. Come now."

Leading Hằng into the biggest bedroom, Co-ra smiles so huge the girl begins to panic. On the bed lie two sleeveless dresses, with see-through skin-color fabric sewn on to make long sleeves. Two pairs of skin-color socks that also cover undergarments. Hằng has heard her mother talk of such a thing but never seen one up close.

She touches the long socks. Smooth and stretchy, thin as breaths. Also there are two scarves, one green, one yellow, from fabric she knows is chiffon. Two pairs of boots await on the floor.

"I stayed up all night fashioning ways to show skin without showing skin, and not to toot my own horn, but I dare someone to come up with fancier outfits." Co-ra takes off her robe and signals for Hằng to do the same. "Me and you, matching from head to toe. Won't folks be tickled?"

Co-ra holds up a yellow dress and asks, "Recognize this?"

Of course, En-Di brought it for Hằng to wear in front of a judge. An exposed dress reconfigured into skin-hiding day wear. Hằng is so impressed with Co-ra's ingenuity she mimics every one of Co-ra's many, many steps in putting on one item after another.

"My mama, now, she never threw out a thing. She didn't grow up with much so she took to saving, just in case. Look how smart she was. I've got a slip and hosiery and a bra and a belt for your tiny self."

Hằng is distracted and forgets to shield the jumble of red lines coursing beneath her skin. It helps that Co-ra fails to react, as if such lines run beneath everybody's skin.

Everything on, Co-ra steps back to inspect. "We are scrumptious. That cousin of yours has great taste. You do splendidly in a flouncy, floral summer dress that adds the illusion of a fuller figure and accentuates your waist. I do declare, at times I think I've missed my calling to become a hairdresser or a fashion designer."

For the final touch, Cora glides something sweet on the girl's lips. "Now, take a peek."

At a full-length mirror, Hằng's eyes burn. Her head shakes

on its own, trying to erase a vision so unexpected she might as well have grown wings.

"What's the matter? You look so pretty."

Hằng can't control her tears or her palms rising to scrub off colors and features that for the first time resemble her mother's. "Nô, khen nót lúc bờ-rít-ti."

She pulls at the stretchy skin on her arms, her legs. It won't tear.

Co-ra yells for Linh. "David, go fetch LeeRoy, now." With a soothing voice, she faces Hằng: "Come sit, it's all right. You don't have to wear anything you don't want."

Hằng runs into the bathroom. Her heart pounds inside her ears but soon Ly-Roi's familiar buzzes claim attention from the other side of the locked door. Co-ra joins him, in speed and volume. They must think her shockingly rude. After all, Co-ra has lost sleep designing the dresses and is willing to stretch make-believe skin over her own arms and legs to soothe Hằng's anticipated panic.

How will Hằng explain she wasn't thinking, only reacting to an image that conflicted with Bà's many warnings still palpitating inside Hằng's skull.

Beauty brings danger. Outside our house, avert others' eyes. Do not laugh, do not pout. You have reached the age. No longer show calves, thighs, arms. No one can protect you should your stare, your walk, flame attention, provoke interest. Remember, leave your hair short, leave your face plain, the more colorless, the better to hide.

No matter how she scrubs, traces of stubborn color cling to her face—glowy cheeks and pink lips, shiny soft hair, pupils so dark they ignite. Hằng keeps staring and can't believe it. No one prepared her for resembling Mother while Father was alive. Back then Mother laughed, gossiped with customers who arrived until dusk to buy beauty potions.

Mother had brows lilted at mid length, lips glossy as if always eating fat, cheekbones infused with rushing blood, hair cascading in black blue. Hằng assumed she could never look like that. After the war, no one wanted to. Mother watered down her face, yet the outside world still brought the unwanted.

Hằng understands she's no longer living after the war. And yet, is it safe to be pretty? Does she want to be pretty? Perhaps in this dry land that reminds her of nothing her past can be locked inside exactly that, the past. Here no one knows her, much less her mother, or her family, or her last six years. They see her and she looks like herself. Inside such a face she might have time to shuffle her history and reveal only her present, for as long as she needs.

A knock. "H?"

She tugs gently at the fabric under which red lines lie quiet. Ly-Roi will have questions.

"Can I see?" In his voice a lightness, as if requesting to see her is as simple as looking at the moon. "It can't be that bad. Any dress at all has got to be better than them dirty pants that has been swallowing you whole."

He laughs. Steady and pleasant as corn popping.

Hằng steps away from the mirror. From four steps back it's difficult to tell where her real skin ends and the artificial one begins. From five back maybe Ly-Roi will forget what he saw.

He calls out, "Let me see you. Cora says you look darling."

"Du gô."

With him gone, she can marvel at arms, legs that haven't been exposed to sunlight since grade school. She remembers the heat, the wind on her skin while in a school uniform of blue skirt and white blouse or while running in shorts and T-shirts. And she's amazed at what's on her feet. Her toes can't wiggle, calves are heated, but Hằng is starting to understand why Ly-Roi yearns to be a cowboy. In such boots, she can stomp on almost anything, even miniature balls of spikes, and manage to retain beauty.

"H, what's the point of making me go? I'm gonna see you soon enough at the fair, right?" He sounds hurt.

She softens her voice. "Du gô, Ai phó-lô."

A long pause before his boot steps fade.

Hằng opens the door. Co-ra stands ready to wipe, reapply, reflutter, refluff. The tube of sweetness gets put inside a purse, its strap crosses Hằng's body. Hằng adds her small notebook and a pencil.

One last time Cora adjusts the handkerchief. "Not a thing is wrong with being pretty. When I was your age, I loved dressing up and drove my mama crazy with crimson lipstick. You clean up real nice, and boys are bound to notice. That's fine as long as they're respectful. Now then, you ready?"

"Ré-đi." Hằng forces a smooth tone, even though her nerves are entangled knowing Ly-Roi awaits outside. She must keep five steps from his knowing eyes.

Bướm Vàng

On account of H, LeeRoy drops a whole crate of cantaloupes. Mr. Morgan comes running, surely hollering. LeeRoy hears none of it. His limbs might as well be dipped in tar, his eyes bulging like a Chihuahua's.

H has been scrubbed into a bona fide pretty girl. Short hair smoothed around her face, and those shiny plump lips, who on earth thought to do that to him? A stirring starts in Wranglers that are loose on him now, thank God. For cover he picks up the crate and strategically places it below his waist. Not one melon has busted.

Mr. Morgan shakes his head, grabs hold of the crate. Lee-Roy thinks of pus and mildew and mold. Surely one day his jeans won't give him away every time he thinks a girl is pretty.

Mr. Morgan seems to be fighting between getting mad

and calming down. "Not ruining my name selling mishandled goods." A sigh, as if the boss man's learning to accept one of life's many irritations. "We'll eat these, get another crate. Careful."

LeeRoy walks away, not trusting the calm. First, he was able to dodge the bullet with H, then Mr. Morgan is all diplomatic like. Something is brewing, and he has a sinking feeling it will land like a Galveston hurricane.

At the fair, people flashing cash are already lined up at the booth. Mr. Morgan hurries with the banner, *Magical Melons*, and it's cattle to Texas bluegrass. Cora and H stay clean and dry, playing smiley cashiers, while the three of them haul, unpack, and stack and sweat. LeeRoy, in his best cowboy getup, would surrender his brand-new hat if it meant standing around and nodding while folks gush about the sweetest, juiciest, firmest cantaloupes ever.

Nothing but grunt work. LeeRoy has a mind to join David's foul mood. The boy has been brooding since seeing no other kid dressed up in khaki shorts and a blue pullover with a collar.

"Ma, you've turned me into a fool."

She came right back. "Hush, other boys wish they look as good as you."

LeeRoy's not at all interested in the tug-of-war between

mother and son. Though they do distract him from a full-on stare at H. The silver belt is a nice touch. The sun glows on her smooth arms. How did Cora get rid of all them red lines? Not that he would bring it up.

Just about every customer is paying thirty dollars for a whole crate, writing on their names for reclaiming later. Mr. Morgan arches his brows at LeeRoy. "Told you."

"All right, all right, I was wrong." It's heating up now, making LeeRoy all the more sticky and grumpy. "If folks are willing to pay for sirloins and get melons, who am I to judge?"

Mr. Morgan looks too smug for his own good. "Mark my word, this won't be the only time I say, 'Told you.'"

"What else you gonna get us selling?" LeeRoy has had about enough of this ranch life. Red will go into the shop tomorrow, then it'll be time to go. But where?

The question rattles him so much it's easier to stand tall against Mr. Morgan, who spews one more warning. "You're gonna wish what's bound to descend on you is as simple as selling something, son."

Spreading that mystery, and having whipped up an unusually tall pile of words, Mr. Morgan strips off his gloves and releases music into the world: "Run off."

Cora puts in her bit. "Y'all stay together. David, I mean it, you can't run off by yourself."

"Mama, I'm eleven."

"Exactly." She hands him ten dollars. "Don't spend it all on sweets. Remember how sick you got last year? And save room for my picnic."

"Ma!"

Cora turns to LeeRoy. "Keep an eye on him, will ya? I know I don't have to worry about her, she'll be glued to her brother."

Behind the booth, H smiles deep enough to show that right dimple. "Ré-đi?"

She's asking her brother, but LeeRoy pipes up. "Ready." He feels jittery for no reason.

David, running ahead, turns back toward them. "C'mon, I saw a sign for fried Snickers." His blue shirt gets tossed.

They tag along, leg-length apart, as David zips from booth to booth gobbling up fried anything. Twinkie, HoHo, Rice Krispie, tamale, jalapeno, popcorn, pickle, licorice. That kid would chow down metal if it was fried. LeeRoy finds himself looking, but not looking, her way. Those lips of hers sparkle. For H's part, she finds every little thing her brother does fascinating.

H gets close to witness the boy lick a fried cherry popsicle. When LeeRoy inches up, H steps back. He's wondering if BO got ahold of him. Sniffs, nope, he's good. Then what is her deal? Maybe being pretty makes her shy.

David looks up and shouts, "Ferris wheel! Broke down before I got a turn last year. Run y'all."

H takes off too. LeeRoy has had enough exercise to get through fall and winter. When he catches up to them, H steps away. David is in line, pointing at a sign: *$1 a ride. 12 and under FREE.*

"It's on me, H." Heat rises up his neck. It's not like they're on a date. Just a gentlemanly thing to do. LeeRoy reaches for his wallet and finds nothing. His whole face catches on fire. "I must have left it in my work pants, sorry. David, I'll pay you back, I swear."

The boy holds out one sweaty dollar.

"You've done soaked up that much grease? Your belly is gonna have many regrets." LeeRoy turns to H. She shakes her head and shows the inside of her purse. Nothing but a pink tube and her notebook.

LeeRoy has to cowboy up. "Y'all go on. I'll watch from here."

"No, you gotta ride." David panics.

H points at her brother. "Hi gô, Ai gô."

They're at the front of the line. The ticket man seems friendly and reasonable enough.

"Mister, see, my wallet—" LeeRoy gets cut off.

"Two dollars, boy's free."

"We got but a one, let me owe you a dollar and I'll bring you two right after. My wallet—"

The ticket man looks bored. "Next."

LeeRoy points at H. "She's twelve, all dressed up today but I swear she's twelve."

H tilts her head. The man lifts a brow. "You reckon he's telling the truth?"

LeeRoy steps toward H. She backs up. He tries again. She backs up. He grabs her arm. "Will you stay put?" Then he notices the thin sleeve and pulls on it. "Cool."

H, wide-eyed and still, looks to be bracing for something bad. He leans closer, nervous himself. "Your dress is pretty, really. C'mon, H, tell the man, 'I reckon so.'"

H shakes her head. That about figures.

"You'll charm him, a Vietnamese girl saying 'reckon so,' trust me, we'll get a freebie out of this."

"Du sây réc-cần."

"It's not cute if a good ol' boy says it. Haven't you heard of the element of surprise?"

H is having none of it, yanks her arm free.

The man sighs. "Folks are waiting. Move along now."

H looks at her brother, who, bless him, mouths, "I reckon so."

A Texas accent flies out her mouth. "Ai réc-cần sô."

"Good 'nuff." The man laughs and tips his hat. "Hell, all y'all get to ride."

David dances around like we saved a hundred, instead of a dollar. Waiting to get on, he would not stand next to his sister, wanting LeeRoy in the middle. The girl puts herself in the middle. David slips to the other side of LeeRoy. They probably look like they all got ants in their pants.

"Will y'all cut it out?" Thank the Lord it's their turn. LeeRoy climbs on first, dragging David after him. H pops right in. The door closes and they're jerked forward. Stop, jerk, stop, jerk. Like riding a possessed roller coaster.

David licks up the last of his batter-dipped popsicle. LeeRoy cain't fathom fried ice, but no one is asking him. Every jerk drips more red stains on David's hands, white undershirt, shorts. He eyes LeeRoy. "Want some?"

"That'd be a big no."

The kid doesn't offer the slobbering mess to H, and LeeRoy wishes he had been extended the same courtesy. She's smiling at her brother, inches away, like she might reach out and pet him. The canyon opens beneath them as they climb to ten o'clock on the wheel.

"Even more amazing from up here, don't ya think?" LeeRoy gets nothing in reply.

H stares at David, who points the popsicle stick in the direction of the ranch.

"I'm going to live there forever." He sounds so sure. LeeRoy wishes he were a kid again, when wanting something was as good as getting it. "Me and Linh, we're gonna have our own ranch and I aim to breed quarter horses."

"Ai gô ghoe du gô." She beams at her brother. An awkward silence. LeeRoy isn't sure he should be repeating "I go where you go," seeing as the boy looks downright alarmed.

All of a sudden David sucks in a breath. On his outstretched hand, sticky with red juice, a yellow butterfly has landed. They all try to stop breathing. There's powder on its wings, opening and closing. Its needle-thin front legs tap back and forth.

David twitches. "It tickles." The butterfly takes off.

H peers into her brother with so much hope LeeRoy is scared for her. *"Bướm vàng."* She points at the zigzagging spot of yellow in the air.

"What?" David asks.

Just like that, she sings.

Kìa con bướm vàng, kìa con bướm vàng . . .

LeeRoy heard it before, on the long, bumpy ride home after a rookie mistake that damn near cost him a chance at fatherhood. For sure he won't be telling his folks about that misfortune. Hell, he can't even clue himself in on what he aims to do with his future. Not a cowboy, that's for sure. Then what? He's starting to feel like a fake and a liar.

H's still singing the melody everybody knows. LeeRoy adds his bit.

Are you sleeping, are you sleeping, Brother John, Brother John?
Morning bells are ringing, morning bells are ringing.
Ding-ding-dong, ding-ding-dong.

David laughs. "So that's the song." He hums. As he hums, H starts up again.

Kìa con bướm vàng, kìa con bướm vàng.

David repeats "*bướm vàng*" clear as day. His expression says it all: he's as surprised as they are.

H gets in his face. "Du rì-mém-bờ?"

He shrugs.

"He remembers what?" LeeRoy asks.

"Áo-ờ xoong." It's good to see H flushed and delighted.

"Y'all have a song?"

H nods. "Bất-tờ-phờ-lai dé-lô."

"Butterfly yellow? You mean yellow butterfly."

H starts to explain but pulls out her notebook. The most prepared notetaker on earth. Bướm = butterfly, vàng = yellow.

She looks like she might hug her brother. 'Course she

doesn't. She does squeeze his arm, imprinting marks. David lets her hold on for a good while before shaking her off. She writes and sings some more. Kìa con bướm vàng = look at butterfly yellow.

She puts her pencil down and points one finger up and down. Darndest thing, David follows exactly, repeating "*bướm vàng.*" Pencil gets to scratching again. Xòe đôi cánh = spread pair wings

Her arms flutter like wings. So do his. Tung cánh bay lên thăm trời = fling wings fly up visit sky.

Their arms twirl above their heads. Em ngồi xem = I sit watch.

With prayer hands, they press one cheek, then the other. Guess the kid remembers something. Both are smiling huge and only at each other. LeeRoy feels like a third wheel.

Translated word for word, LeeRoy understands it has to be butterfly yellow, adjective following noun. Same syntax as Spanish, *mariposa amarilla*, and probably a whole lot of languages.

LeeRoy calls on a version learned in Beginner Spanish. David sings too.

Buenos días, buenos días
Cómo estás, cómo estás?

Muy bien, gracias, muy bien, gracias,
Ding-dang-dong, ding-dang-dong.

H rocks her newly smooth head, amused. LeeRoy can't believe this is the same face that glared at him all summer. Instead of a full-tilt nervousness, he looks at her and feels a jittery warmth pulsating in his gut. He does like looking at her.

H starts something like "Frère Jacques, Frère Jacques." LeeRoy laughs and joins her.

Dormez-vous, dormez-vous?
Sonnez les matines, sonnez les matines, Ding-dang-
        dong, ding-dang-dong.

Rising to twelve o'clock, two at a time are able to sing in a constant loop of Vietnamese, English, Spanish, French. At the top, the wheel stops altogether. A breeze swings their passenger tub just so. No tiny person down in the blasted heat could guess that it's cool and shaded where they sit. The land expands until one horizon edges against hills, another against tall greens, yet another going on and on into the canyon striped in gray, yellow, maroon, lavender, orange, red. They all sigh. The wheel stays put to let them soak in their fill.

The Horrid and the Sublime

Hằng knows she should be elated. Her brother remembered "*bướm vàng*," pronouncing it with the northern accent Bà taught him. He let Hằng clutch his arm. Their first real words, first touch. They all sang. They all laughed. Just a moment ago she joined in their lightness.

Now at the highest point, staring into a canyon aglow in colors, her heart sinks. It's hard to admit she's disappointed. Even if she tells Linh every story in the notebook, he will not come away with her. His horse, his ranch, his mama, his room, his friends, his school. An abundant life. After six years and four months of plotting expecting saving hoping, she must accept Linh requires no rescue.

The more Hằng stares into the immense tear in the earth, the more she sees a dusty, wind-beaten ocean floor. Ly-Roi said millions of years ago this canyon was an ocean. Now wildflowers flutter in the colors of tropical fish. Heat waves resemble sea plants. Brown grass spreads like seaweed across the expanse. Buried within such a floor must be countless bones, leaves, shapes belonging to lives that long ago drifted and flourished. Maybe not all flourished; maybe some were flung in and joined the immense burial ground at the bottom of the sea.

Her mother is down there. More than likely she will dissolve into the salt, the currents. Each hair, each vein, each morsel of flesh, of skin shredded and nibbled until she turns diaphanous. But perhaps a bone, a long bone or a short bone, will lodge against a rock and be imprinted.

Millions of years from now, when the sea between Việt Nam and Thái Lan has evaporated to dust, perhaps a hiker will find a trace of Mother among fossilized recordings of what was.

Would Mother say crossing the sea was worth it? Most likely. Those years spent softening to noodles in her bed, she whispered in a circle, *"We have to know, we have to know."* Now Hằng knows her brother doesn't need her. Not the way she needs him to fuel her days.

Linh has become someone she can't imagine. A blankness obscures details of his present. Favorite fruit, best friend, does he dream, when did he last cry? It's pointless to push. He won't reveal his present self unless she waits.

Bà would wait. An expert at waiting, she would maneuver a life beside Linh and cook and eat and talk and reminisce. Hằng understands she will have hours beside Linh. But what else?

Ly-Roi and Linh are laughing. Always a lightness between them and from them. Maybe without war people do flit around fluffy as birds, their wants equal their needs equal their present equals their future. But then Bà always said the only constant in life is impermanence.

It's exhausting, the incessant flip of emotions. On the island, after the last slithering of worms, Hằng yearned to sit alone and be horrified. Surely the other girl did too. But there was chopping and sizzling until both girls were offered plates of food arranged like paintings.

On a shiny banana leaf sat a purple sea creature full of thorns, its egg-sized hard shell halved to reveal raw golden glistening lumps. A white orchid speckled with brown hovered beside a grilled fish. A light yellow paste released the unmistakable spicy clutch of mashed wild ginger.

Both girls received chopsticks of twigs. Many eyes watched, many hands labored. They must eat.

A dab of ginger on a golden lump from the same spiny creature that had punctured her flesh every time waves thrashed her against rocks. Salty briny sea on her tongue, dissolving when pressed against the roof of her mouth. Nutty, and once swallowed, there lingered an unlikely sweetness. She let the other lump sit longer on awakened taste buds.

It seemed implausible after pirates and holes and worms she should be granted a meal so sublime.

The other girl agreed, giggling as she savored the same ginger and gold. She waved the orchid and vanilla bloomed.

"From now on my name is Lan (Orchid)," the girl said.

Hằng did not ask about her previous name. Did not ask about her back.

The girl said, *"It tastes like nothing I know."* She tucked the orchid in her hair. *"My name is Lan and I'm going to live with my aunt in Australia and my life starts today and I don't remember yesterday or any days before."*

Hằng did not ask how she was able to forget. Maybe Lan would achieve the shiny life Hằng's aunt talked of. College, husband, house, vacations, cars, clothes, children glossy of skin and worthy of brags.

Only one day to have old horrors flip her sublime concentration.

The incessant flips. Thorn-infested mesquites turned into smooth horse carvings in Ông Mó-gần's hands. Stretchy sleeves certain to incite a cyclone of questions inspired one indecipherable word from Ly-Roi: "Cool." A plump-palm, wordy cowboy evolved into a being who joined her inhales, her exhales.

Even pirates marinating the cruelest thoughts had someone with whom they shared kindness. Did their mothers, fathers, wives, children, brothers, sisters know?

If Hằng indulges, she could spend every second engorged in anger. Linh provided a shield, forced upon her an outside intensity. If Hằng doesn't have him, she might cling to vengeance. Bà could have too. Her husband, her son. But Bà believed life is long, the universe will deliver justice, eventually. Bà chose to cultivate a life. Steered her sons from becoming soldiers, tended to her garden, stared into love and hate, beauty and ugliness, joy and anguish, healing and pain. To seek one is to accept the other, like chopsticks. *Cái gì cũng có đôi, everything has a pair.*

At any time in any place an act of horror is being committed. At any time in any place an act of sublimity is being felt. Each circulating, sniffing the other like dogs, but one cannot destroy the other. The fatty burn of worms shared the air with the orchid's vanilla.

The other girl held her smile. So charming that when a rescue helicopter appeared a day later, with UNHCR bright and bold on its belly, a gaunt man in eyeglasses and a white shirt did not believe in the girl's emergency. It did not help that Lan kept telling him she fell into the cooking fire. The herbalist pulled the man aside and explained, sighed, described, insisted until the girl and Hằng were flown out first. A boat was sent for the rest of the stranded.

The girls were expedited to the last-stage refugee processing camp in Bataan, Philippines, where again they were fast-tracked to fly out of Manila after four and a half months. Other escapees were envious, having waited much longer, months later to turn into years. The girls only whispered that they had relatives eager to pay for their airfares. They did not explain their folders were stamped with "Extreme Trauma."

Someone shakes Hằng. "You okay, H?"

She stares at Ly-Roi and holds her head still. Leaning across her brother, he peers into her with the same soft concern he showed at the canyon. A slight shake of her head. A light nod from his. They understand and that's enough for now.

A gust blows his mustache into his mouth. She smiles and he seems relieved for her.

"Sometimes they're more trouble than they're worth."

David pulls on one end. "When I grow up, I'm gonna grow one."

"NÔ!" Her alarm escapes loudly. The other two look at her for an explanation, but they're back on the ground. She walks on ahead. Dry, firm earth. So much of it that Hằng could walk for days in her new boots and never have to touch a lake, a river, an ocean. Walk for days across a land that is the opposite of a lush tropical island, a land where dust and blankness might allow her to thaw. Bà gone, Father gone, Mother gone. Not yet, but soon, she imagines sinking inside the indulgence of mourning.

Her brother runs past her to a booth, waving his last dollar.

Ly-Roi comes to her side. He doesn't seem offended by her loud "NÔ." Maybe he means it, and the flying caterpillars could be relinquished. She tries to see his face hairless. She would like it.

He takes off his cowboy hat and hovers it above her as they walk.

"Du cao-bồi." She points at him.

"No H, it's time I hang it up. I'm no more a cowboy than you are."

Quivers claim his voice. She understands him all the better for feeling disappointment, for wanting something out of reach. "Du o ấy ri-eo cao-bồi chu mi."

He smiles a sad smile. "It does have a nice ring to it. 'You are a real cowboy to me.' And don't think I didn't notice you saying 'are' and 'a.'"

She has been practicing *be* verbs and articles. She will get them right.

She nudges the hat back on his head.

Silence

He has the both of them for one more day. The tall boy, antsy as can be, is out mucking. Then fences, prairie dog holes, troughs, salt blocks, hay. If all is good, he'll take the boy to pay for his truck and that should be the last of him.

The girl he's got with him. They're shoveling buckets of rich black foam from composted banana peels. He found his son's kid shovel for her. Works fine. She can lift a full bucket as well as any ranch hand.

He's tied a string to his finger to remember more bananas. Sometimes the grocer hands over overripe ones and thanks him for hauling them away.

He hasn't told a soul Mildred's secret. She did agree if their son wants the ranch, then he could be told. So far, his son likes his fancy city life fighting injustice, as if there isn't plenty of injustice right at home. Every Christmas he brings his sleek self home for two weeks and goes right back.

About broke his mama's heart. She passed five years ago. He finds he talks to her as much as he ever did, late at night, just the two of them in the dark. He tells her again she saved their ranch, tells her he was blessed.

Four buckets at a time ride in a barrel. He's getting on in years. The girl takes hold of one handle and he the other as they push toward the clean-out beds. All yesterday they pulled down vines and stored the stakes and turned the tired soil. He has never let ranch hands tend to the cantaloupes. They talk. They're nosy.

The girl he doesn't mind. Her best work habit is her ability to stay quiet.

After every bed gets two inches of compost, he'll sit her with him on the tractor and make trips to the manure piles. Come spring there won't be anything better for cantaloupes.

It was a bad drought when his daddy gave him the ranch handed down from his daddy and went and died. No wheat that year, no hay either. Mildred didn't know a thing about wheat but she knew cantaloupes. Everyone from Pecos had that in their veins. Started working the fields when she was knee high. There, the potassium was right in the soil to yield a big fruit, and local water had plenty of salt to retain water and work up juice.

Mildred was so proud. Came up with the beds to save

watering. Came up with potassium from composting banana peels, seeing as sweet potatoes were too good to waste. Milk and white beans they needed to get through the days. When her father said to use avocados they laughed. Nobody was going to let avocados rot.

His secret is adding salt to the water, had always done so before first light. It does get tiring hauling buckets. The salt level has to be just right: too much and sugar gets diluted, too little and you get cucumbers. A week before harvesting is rest time. No watering at all so the sweetness can concentrate.

They're done. The girl is picking from her bed. A whole lot going on. Green beans and celery and kale are what he can name. She plucks a long thin leaf and holds it out to him.

He starts to taste it but she shakes her head. Breaks the leaf and brings it to his nose. How about that, ginger. Who knew the entire plant smells like the rhizomes? She digs in the soil and out come stubby fingers. There's not a whole lot on his ranch he hasn't seen. Ginger out of the ground is one.

She's picked enough. He helps carry leaves and waves her toward his kitchen.

He washes the ginger and minces it fine. Puts it in a few cups of water, set to boil. Adds sugar, molasses, and salt. Lets it cool.

Meanwhile she's gone to Cora's and come back in clothes more fitting to a girl like her who's no bigger than a foal. She gestures toward his soup pot, his oil, his garlic. Sure. She washes and cuts her pile of leaves as tender as tending a baby.

The smell brings back Mildred. She never boiled her vegetables, did something fancy called a sauté and it was good. It's been a long time since he put a garden in his belly.

He gets up and pulls the bubble water from the fridge. A good third glass of ginger syrup, maybe she likes it sweet, and pours in the bubbles. Makes another for himself.

He tells her the idea on his mind since talking to Cora.

"I need a gardener. A hundred dollars a month, all year."

"Mi?"

"Yes you. Wouldn't have anyone else."

She blinks, not believing him. He nods. She nods. It's done. They clink glasses. The boy comes in, looks at the girl wide-eyed, doesn't hear the offer of a ginger ale.

"Let's take yours to the porch." They leave the girl to her vegetables.

The boy's hand shakes as he drinks. It's his heart. The first time always feels like a loft of hay fell on you.

"You'll be all right, son. You picked a good one."

"You know?"

"All along."

"What's with me?"

"I'm not going to ruin it for you by naming it. I had mine.

Far as I'm concerned that's the best reason for opening your eyes in the morning. She's done gone on. But I'm grateful, son. I got to look at her for a long time."

"What do I do?"

"You already know."

The boy starts to protest.

"You about ready to go get your truck?"

Color comes back to his face. "Yes, sir."

It's downright red when he asks if she can come along.

"I figured as much."

Surprise

Red looks great. Nothing but sleek new paint. Worth every penny except all he's got left is sixty dollars.

H looks even better, but LeeRoy can't be whooping about her out in the open. Fitted jeans, a blouse with fluttery sleeves, a yellow handkerchief at her neck. When he first saw her wearing that in Mr. Morgan's kitchen, his heart flared. He's got it under control now, even if looking at her still jitters his nerves.

Mr. Morgan is about to take H back to the ranch when LeeRoy pulls the boss man aside.

"I'm kinda wanting to ask her to lunch."

The man grins.

"Not a date or nothing, but we gotta celebrate Red's full recovery." LeeRoy knows he's talking too much. "Besides, my mama helped put together a surprise for her."

"Is that right?"

When H agrees to lunch, it's good that Mr. Morgan drives off and takes his grin with him.

H springs it on him while smoothing her palm across Red's vanished old wound. She's going to live with Cora and cook dinner for room and board and tend to Mr. Morgan's garden for a hundred a month.

"I figured you'd live with your uncle."

"Mai bờ-ró-đờ he-rè." She says it like that's news.

"Yeah, but what are you going to be doing?"

"Ai lớp vé-ghi-ta-bồ."

"Love vegetables enough to be a gardener?"

"Ai ha-vờ mo bờ-lans."

"What plans?" He notices her *s* came out soft as can be.

H smiles huge like it's the best secret in the world. He'll get it out of her later.

It seems everybody has a plan except for him. He's got a mighty nice truck and enough money for two sandwiches and maybe a full tank of gas. He was wanting to take her to that steakhouse but he can't fathom trying for a free seventy-two-ounce steak anymore.

"You hungry, H?"

"Ai ít quít Ông Mó-gân."

LeeRoy doesn't want to seem too pleased, but that means

one sandwich and for sure a full tank.

H doesn't seem bothered by a thing. The wind blowing her short strands and her face has hills of bones and valleys of sunken cheeks. A face he'd never imagined before this summer has become a face he sees with eyes closed.

He pops in his cousin's cassette. Blondie's "Rapture." H likes it, her fingers drumming her thigh. All of a sudden she takes a tube out of her purse and starts glossing her lips. Those darn plump lips.

"H, uh, maybe don't do that right now?"

"Goai?"

Always why with her. He's not about to explain. Better to think of armadillos flattened and stinking all over this open land. Best yet, just get her to her surprise.

The bookstore at West Texas State was easy enough to find. Getting her to actually set foot in there is another story. Out of the truck, H ran to a tree, then stopped dead to watch a bunny before it hid under a bush. Now they're reading about a statue of a woman with her hair in a bun.

"That's Georgia O'Keefe, my mama loves her stuff. Says here she taught in the art department from 1916 to 1918 when this was West Texas State Normal College. I had no idea there's a university right close to Amarillo."

"A-ma-ri-lo?"

"No, it's Amarillo. 'Course real Spanish speakers probably cringe at how we say it."

"Em-ma-rí-lô?"

"Yeah. It means yellow, like your scarf."

Her scarf is so light and pretty. A lot of things about her are light and pretty.

H mumbles "Amarillo" and "yellow" to herself. LeeRoy thinks about the university right here, how his parents might be impressed with the Georgia O'Keefe angle. But they'll ask what's his major and he can't say pronunciation coach. Can he? He's gonna think this through.

He drags H to the bookstore. "You'll like it, I promise. My mama went through a little trouble to find it and have it shipped here, but she can talk folks into giving her their skin if she wanted."

"Do ma-ma?"

LeeRoy flushes. "I mean, it's no big deal. She'd do this for anybody."

H seems to believe him.

The book is waiting. He makes H turn around while he writes an inscription. His mama insisted on that, so years from now his sentiment will still be sitting on a shelf waiting for her.

"Here you go. *Handy Pocket Guide to Tropical Fruits.*"

She holds it, flips through colorful photographs, then lets out a squeal like she's being tortured. They leave.

Outside, she points to the name of a round purple fruit with a green clover-leaf hat.

"I guess that'd be mangosteen."

She's jumping up and down. *"Trái măng cụt."*

"Try man kut?" It's hopeless. But she doesn't have time to scold him, points to a red round bunch with a second picture of white translucent flesh. She points to its name.

"L-y-c-h-e-e. I guess that'd be lee-chee?"

"Trái vải." Now she points to "starfruit" and says *"trái khế,"* to "guava" and says *"trái ổi,"* to "jackfruit" and says *"trái mít."*

"I'm glad to know all this, but looking at food is making me so hungry I might start licking your pages. You wouldn't want that."

H, being H, is not done. She points to "persimmon" and says *"trái hồng,"* to "durian" and says *"trái sầu riêng,"* to "cherimoya" and says *"trái na."*

He has to lift her finger off the page. That means he's holding her hand. There's a quick jolt, like a shock. Her palm is softer than he thought, even after working like a donkey all summer.

"You should know by now I can't tolerate being hungry." He looks around. There's pizza. "Let's walk over there and you can tell me all them names until your throat goes dry. Okay?"

She takes back her hand to hug the book as they walk. Still, their hands did touch for a good bit.

H & L

Before Ly-Roi leaves, her brother insists that he and Hằng smell Linh the Horse. She can't decline, and neither can Ly-Roi. They touch their noses to brown fur. In the waist of her jeans is the fruit book. She's careful to not let it touch the horse.

Ly-Roi pulls away within three counts. "It smells like a horse."

Her brother is tense. "You didn't take a good enough sniff."

They both try again while Linh's words stretch over them. "Every horse has its own smell, like people. Don't you smell something really good, like mac and cheese?"

"I smell sweat and hay and yes, poop."

Her brother blows a breath, looks at her to make it up to him. A deep inhale. Earth after rain, leaves in the sun, cinnamon powder, raw meat. All pulsating of heat.

"Vé-ri gút."

Linh doesn't seem any happier. "Very good how?"

She points to the land itself. "Lai đất."

Linh the Boy shakes his head and plunges his face into Linh the Horse. Then he sniffs the air and looks more agitated. "Nope, nothing alike."

Ly-Roi rescues her. "Remember when I talked about the NFR championship? I might be coming around here on the way there."

The sun opens on her brother's face. "Will you take me?"

Ly-Roi hesitates until Linh speaks up. "She can come too, I guess. Mama and Mr. Morgan went a long time ago."

They both look at her, waiting. "Ai gô chu."

Ly-Roi tries to hide a smile before turning to Linh. "December then, kid."

Her brother gets on his horse from a stump, as easily as swinging his leg over a chair. "Take it easy."

Hằng knows her good-bye won't be as easy. She and Ly-Roi walk to Red. He opens the truck door and starts to say something and stops.

She yells, "Sập-rais!"

On the passenger seat, Hằng had sneaked a bag of celery, washed and cut.

"Celery? Thanks, H."

He doesn't sound sufficiently surprised or grateful. "Phom mai ga-đần."

The celery took months of planning: asking for seeds, then planting and nurturing until harvest.

"From your garden? Wow, that's very thoughtful."

Hằng keeps her narrowed eyes on him until he says, "Really, very thoughtful. Thank you so much."

She's pleased and points to twenty dollars tucked under the bag. She owes it to him. Besides, she will save much more for emergency money. Her uncle will pay for classes, a condition for her living here, along with a promise that she and Linh will visit his family for Tết.

"Aw, no H, I can't take that. I already owe you three hundred for Red. C'mon, no."

He shoves the bill back in her palm. They hold hands. An electrical current, much stronger than earlier. They drop hands.

She needs to slow her heart with talk about anything. "Ai gô chu sờ-cun."

"Really? Which school?"

"Con-vờ-sấy-sần-nồ Inh-lích."

"That's a great idea. Then everybody will understand you, not that you don't talk well now. I mean everybody can use a course in Conversational English to, I guess, learn how to talk better."

His nervousness matches hers.

"Ai sтớ-dì . . ." She stops talking and draws in the air what she'll also be studying.

"A drawing class? That's a great idea. That's good. I wouldn't want you waiting around for your brother. I mean, nothing wrong with wanting to be with him. But you should have your own thing going."

She has grown accustomed to his face. A kind face, and her cousin is right, a handsome face. She tries not to blush.

"Bai-bai." She doesn't mean to say bye. "Nót bai." She's not making sense.

He doesn't know what to say either. He lingers then reaches out and clutches her right arm. Something like a quarter of a hug.

"Bye then, H."

He gets in the truck. She yells out, "Bai L."

He laughs. "L, I like it." A long breath before he asks, "Did you read what I wrote?" He points to the book tucked in her jeans. He reverses before she looks up.

His truck stirs up dust. Within the cloud, an arm waves out the window until the truck turns and fades into the main roadway. She opens the book. On the first page, under the title that leaves a vast white blankness: YOU SEE, IN THIS WORLD THERE ARE TWO KINDS OF PEOPLE, MY FRIEND. THOSE WHO GO AWAY, AND THOSE WHO COME BACK. I'LL BE BACK.

She giggles at lines remolded from *The Good, the Bad, and the Ugly*, which she and her father cemented in their minds. "You see, in this world there are two kinds of people, my friend. Those with loaded guns, and those who dig. You dig." As she walks back to the spread-out house, her mind floats and meets a lightness. Inside, she has her own room next to her brother, with an identical rectangular window. From there, she can look out and see Ly-Roi drive up in December.

Author's Note

[TK]

Acknowledgments

[TK]

THANHHÀ LẠI

BUTTERFLY YELLOW

BUTTERFLY YELLOW

THANHHÀ LẠI